Sunny Sweet
Is So NOT Scary

Also by Jennifer Ann Mann

Sunny Sweet Is So Not Sorry
Sunny Sweet Is So Dead Meat
Sunny Sweet Can So Get Lost

SUNNY SWEET
Is So NOT Scary

Jennifer Ann Mann

BLOOMSBURY
NEW YORK LONDON OXFORD NEW DELHI SYDNEY

First published in the United States of America in October 2015
by Bloomsbury Children's Books
www.bloomsbury.com

Bloomsbury is a registered trademark of Bloomsbury Publishing Plc

For information about permission to reproduce selections from this book, write to
Permissions, Bloomsbury Children's Books, 1385 Broadway, New York, New York 10018
Bloomsbury books may be purchased for business or promotional use. For information on
bulk purchases please contact Macmillan Corporate and Premium Sales Department at
specialmarkets@macmillan.com

Library of Congress Cataloging-in-Publication Data
Mann, Jennifer Ann, author.
Sunny Sweet is so not scary / by Jennifer Ann Mann.
pages   cm
Summary: Masha, Junchao, and Alice are having a slumber party—with scary movies and
popcorn—but when the lights go out and they start to hear noises they become convinced
that a ghost is in the house, and Masha's brilliant little sister, Sunny, decides that they
should collect actual data on the spirit world and become ghost hunters.
ISBN 978-1-61963-507-4 (hardcover) • ISBN 978-1-61963-508-1 (e-book)
1. Sisters—Juvenile fiction. 2. Best friends—Juvenile fiction. 3. Sleepovers—Juvenile
fiction. 4. Ghost stories. [1. Sisters—Fiction. 2. Genius—Fiction. 3. Best friends—Fiction.
4. Friendship—Fiction. 5. Sleepovers—Fiction. 6. Ghosts—Fiction.] I. Title.
PZ7.M31433St 2015   [Fic]—dc23   2014043363

Book design by John Candell
Typeset by Newgen Knowledge Works (P) Ltd., Chennai, India
Printed and bound in the U.S.A. by Thomson-Shore Inc., Dexter, Michigan
2 4 6 8 10 9 7 5 3 1

All papers used by Bloomsbury Publishing, Inc., are natural, recyclable products
made from wood grown in well-managed forests. The manufacturing processes
conform to the environmental regulations of the country of origin.

To Nayeli Dalton

Sunny Sweet
Is So NOT Scary

Sunny Sweet Is So Not Scary

I'm in charge!" I said.

"Mom said Mrs. Song was in charge," said Sunny.

"Mrs. Song is in charge only in an emergency," I told her. "And watching a movie is not an emergency."

This was my very first sleepover, and I didn't want my little sister hanging out with us the entire night. I was trying to pay more attention to Sunny since we got back from summer camp, and I had already let her stay for crafting (Junchao, Alice, and I made friendship bracelets while Sunny strung DNA strands), karaoke (Sunny sang something she called a gregory chant that went on *forever*), Scrabble (Sunny won with *jonquils*), and painting our nails (Junchao chose purple, Alice chose black, I chose orange, and Sunny melted all our Styrofoam cups with the nail polish remover). It was time for this to be *my* first sleepover and not Sunny's.

"Good night, Sunny," I said.

Sunny hung her little head and walked out of the living room.

Once she was gone, Junchao broke down. "I feel bad for her, Masha. What about letting her stay for the movie?"

"Yeah," said Alice. "And then you can tell her to go to bed. Because you have to admit, the Styrofoam cup thing was kind of cool. What did she say happened? Something about pollywogs?"

"Polymers," said Junchao, "which are long chains of monomers."

"Guys," I said. "Forget Dr. Frankensunny. This sleepover is only for the *Xing Yun San You*," which is what Mrs. Song always called Alice, Junchao, and me.

2

In English it meant the "Lucky Three" because we were three great friends and the number three was lucky in Chinese culture. "Plus," I added, "it's a scary movie, and Sunny doesn't like scary movies."

This was totally true. Sunny didn't like scary movies. Not because she got scared but because none of it was "scientifically possible." The movies annoyed the skinny little genius. And the skinny little genius annoyed me while I was trying to watch them. She always wanted to talk about matter and molecules when all I wanted to do was shout, *"Don't go down into the basement!"*

Alice, Junchao, and I huddled together on the couch with a big bowl of popcorn in front of us. I hugged my cuddly stuffed Eeyore that Alice got me from Disney World and clicked through our choices for the movie. I'd been looking forward to this night with my two best friends ever since I got home from summer camp.

The whole sleepover thing had actually been my mom's idea. She felt so bad about Sunny turning the dude ranch into Camp Newton and my surprise horse

3

turning into my father's new girlfriend, Claudia, that she suggested I have my very first sleepover. But after we planned everything, she was asked to attend a conference for work at the last minute.

It looked like the whole night was off, and I didn't know what was worse—that I wasn't having the sleepover or that I had to tell Alice that I wasn't having the sleepover. Alice flipped out just like I knew she would. She said if I canceled the sleepover that her parents would probably never let her go to another one again because it had taken her a week to convince her mom and dad to let her go to this one. Her parents were mega nervous about Alice needing special stuff because of her spine problems from spina bifida.

But then Mrs. Song saved the day. She said she'd help out with the sleepover and spend the night at our house. Mrs. Song had been a nurse back in China, and that made Alice's parents really happy.

"Okay," I said, "we can watch *Zombie Revolution*, *Creatures of the Mist*, *Soul Snatchers*, or *Dark Poltergeists*."

4

"I choose none of those," Junchao cried. "They sound too scary."

"That's the point." I giggled. But I secretly agreed with Junchao. These movies did sound too scary. But this was what you did at a sleepover. It was required.

Junchao yawned.

"No, no, you can't be tired," I yelled. "It's way too early. We have to stay up all night."

"All night?" asked Junchao. "As in, until my mom picks me up in the morning?"

"Yes, that's the entire point of a sleepover . . . to stay up," I told her.

"I've never done that before," she said. "I don't know if I can."

"Humans are able to stay awake for up to 264 hours, or approximately eleven days," came a voice from behind the armchair. "Although you will show signs of progressive, and possibly significant, deficits in higher mental processes as the duration of sleep deprivation increases." It was Sunny's voice.

"Sunny!" I yelled. "Get out!"

I heard her scamper back to her room.

"Come on, you guys. We can do this," I said.

"Then let's choose *Dark Poltergeists*," Alice suggested. "I heard it was super scary."

"That's the spirit." I laughed. "Get it, spirit?"

"We get it," laughed Alice.

"I don't get it," said Junchao.

"Anyway," I said, "being scared will definitely keep us up."

"That's because the brain's hypothalamus activates both the sympathetic nervous system and the adrenal-cortical system, which make you become tense and alert with an increase in your heart rate and blood pressure, known as the fight-or-flight response."

"SUNNY!" I shouted. "I'm going to tell Mrs. Song."

Again I heard her feet patter back down the hall.

I wasn't really going to bother Mrs. Song. She was already the greatest person ever because she said yes to doing this *and* she'd made us dumplings! I promised myself that no matter what happened, I wasn't waking up Mrs. Song. She had gone to sleep in my mother's bedroom after karaoke.

We shut off all the lights except for the lamp next to the couch, and I started the movie. As the music began and the beginning credits came on, a little story ran on the screen saying that the events were based on a real incident that took place in New Bedford, New Jersey.

"That's not that far from here," Junchao breathed.

"Don't worry. We're all together," I said.

But I was worried. I didn't like that this was a true story and that it happened so close by. I pulled the blanket from the back of the couch and put it around us. Alice took one of Junchao's hands and I took the other. Junchao smiled a little less worried-looking smile. It made me feel better too, and the three of us settled onto the couch.

At first, the movie looked like it was just about a normal family that moves into a new house. But then strange things started to happen. Footsteps echoed down the hall at night. The lights flickered on and off for no reason. And the family heard a strange moaning sound coming from empty rooms in the house. Then a huge storm hit.

7

Lightning flashed across the screen. Thunder rumbled out of the television. All three of us jumped.

The boy from the family woke up, got out of bed, and walked slowly through the dark house—down a looong hallway where an old clock stood *tick, tick, ticking* . . . past a shelf next to books where a doll sat with open, staring eyes . . . through a lonely dining room with lots of empty chairs . . . and then into the kitchen, where he switched on the light.

Junchao snatched the blanket away from us and threw it over her head.

"Nothing happened yet," I said.

"I'm getting ready," she answered, her voice muffled by the blanket.

Then the lights in the boy's kitchen went out, making Alice and me jump.

"What happened?" Junchao asked.

Before we could answer, the light next to our couch went out.

I looked at Alice. Alice's eyes glowed back at me. We dove under the blanket with Junchao.

"What happened? What happened?" asked Junchao.

"The light went out," Alice said.

"Did you see the ghost?" Junchao asked.

Alice gave a yelp, and the two of us practically crawled on top of Junchao at the idea that a ghost had turned off our light.

"*Our* light went out, Junchao. The one next to the couch," I whispered.

Junchao grabbed onto us. "There's a ghost in this house?" she screeched.

"Shh," I told her. I was afraid that if there was a ghost, it would hear her and then it would know that we knew that it was here.

We huddled under the blanket, listening to the storm still raging on the TV. I wondered why the ghost didn't turn that off too. Between two cracks of thunder I heard a tiny giggle.

I yanked the blanket off my head.

"Don't go out there," Junchao cried.

I cleared my throat and then in my best outdoor voice said, "Did you know that the pupils in your eyes constrict in the dark?" Mrs. Hull had taught us all about the human eye in science class last year. I knew

9

that your pupils actually dilated, or grew bigger in the dark. They didn't constrict or get smaller. I also knew that *someone else* knew this.

"That's not true," said that someone else. "Your pupils dilate in the dark, allowing more light to enter the eye, improving your night vision."

Alice and Junchao threw off the blanket.

"Turn on the light, Sunny," I said.

There was silence for a second, and then Sunny said, "It's a ghoooost." Her voice came from behind the window drapes.

"It is not a ghost," I said. "It is a little sister who will be a ghost very soon if she does not turn on the light."

The light did not turn on.

"Sunny, come out from behind the drapes," I said. "It's time for you to go to bed."

"Hoo, hoo, hoo."

"Sunny, that's the sound an owl makes . . . not a ghost!"

"Sunny is sleeepiiing; this is a ghoul-ie ghost. I'm made up of pure energy, not ectoplasm, which isn't even real . . . like me."

I paused the movie, hopped off the couch, and turned the light back on. Then I walked to the window. When I swung the curtain back, there stood Sunny.

"Boo?" she said, smiling.

"You are so *not* scary," I said.

Before Sunny could answer, the door to the basement rattled.

"Masha! Did you hear that?" asked Junchao.

Sunny danced out from behind the drapes. "That was just the flow of gases caused by air moving from high pressure to low pressure. Sometimes it's called wind," she added.

"Did it just get cold in here?" Alice asked.

"Probably your veins under your skin are constricting to send more blood to major muscle groups as part of the fight-or-flight response, since you're scared about the door rattling. Less blood in your skin makes you cold."

There was a *clomp, clomp, clomp* of footsteps coming from somewhere, but I couldn't tell exactly where.

"Mrs. Song?" I called. But somehow I knew that it wasn't Mrs. Song.

"Your veins are definitely constricting now." Sunny giggled.

"Shh," I said. The four of us stood listening . . . listening . . . listening. All was quiet.

Finally, Junchao sighed, Alice leaned back onto the couch, and I dropped into the armchair. It was nothing. I started to breathe again, and even though I tried not to think about it, I thought about the blood running back into the veins in my arms.

Wooo.

We looked at Sunny. Sunny blinked back at us. She hadn't moved or said a word.

Wooo. Woooo.

"What was that?" I asked.

All four of us jumped under the blanket.

Don't Chew Gum in Turkey

"Ghosts aren't real," Sunny said.

"Then why are you under the blanket with us?" I snapped.

"Because you guys jumped under and it looked like fun."

I actually really wanted to believe Sunny. She was a genius. She knew lots of things. She probably knew this too.

"My grandmother says that ghosts are totally real," whispered Alice. Her face was so close to mine under the blanket that it didn't even look like her. I didn't like it. "And my grandmother was born in Turkey, where they know a ton about ghosts. She says that if you chew gum at night, you're actually chewing the flesh of the dead."

"What!" Junchao howled.

"She says . . ."

I put my hand over Alice's mouth. "We heard you," I told her.

"Your babushka is just being superstitious," said Sunny. "That means she believes in things that are mythical and can't be proven by science. I only believe in things that can be upheld using the scientific method, which are ideas that are tested using measurable evidence and based on principles of reasoning."

I was still freaking out over the gum thing, so I wasn't listening to a scientific word Sunny was saying. All I knew was that she said ghosts were not real and I liked that. I also knew that I was sweating a ton under this blanket with everybody breathing.

I peeked out.

14

The light next to the couch lit up the living room. The movie was still paused. Everything looked normal.

"I'm getting out from under this blanket," I said. Sunny and Alice joined me.

The cool air in the room felt great on my face. I breathed in a giant gulp of it as I looked around to be sure that there was no ghost. After about a minute, Junchao sighed and came out too.

"Did you know that Albert Einstein believed in ghosts?" Junchao said. "And he is the most famous scientist." Long strands of her thick black hair were floating up in the air over her head from being under the blanket.

"Albert Einstein did not believe in ghosts," Sunny said.

"He did too," Junchao insisted. "He believed in the law of physics that says that energy can't be created or destroyed but only change form . . . so what happens to our body's energy when we die?"

"My grandmother knows what happens," Alice said. "It becomes a ghost!"

I looked around the room again—scared that Alice just saying the word *ghost* might make it appear. But

15

it didn't. And with the lights on, we all started to relax. Alice picked up a big handful of popcorn and shoved it in her mouth. The sound of her crunching made me think about the gum in Turkey again. I was hoping that the flesh thing applied only to gum and not popcorn.

"The energy does not become a ghost," Sunny said. "Basic physics tells us that after you die, the energy in your body is sucked up by the environment, either by a wild animal that eats you or worms and bacteria that eat you. Then the plants get our energy from the soil."

"Can we stop talking about eating gross things and being eaten by gross things?" I said. "Let's put the movie back on."

"Really?" Junchao asked. "But aren't you still scared?"

"Nope," I said, faking it because I was still scared. But Sunny had said there was no such thing as ghosts. And Sunny was always right. Not that I was *ever* in my entire life going to say that out loud. "Anyway, it's just a movie."

16

"That's true," said Alice. "My mom always says that."

I was glad to hear something Alice's mom said, and not her grandmother.

Junchao still didn't look convinced.

"We'll turn on all the lights," I suggested.

"And we'll hold hands again," Alice said.

"You guys are the best *gui mi* ever," Junchao smiled. *Gui mi* meant "good friend" in Chinese.

"Let's do this thing!" I laughed.

I skipped over to the light switch and flipped on both the lights in the living room and the dining room. On my way back to the couch I thought I heard something. It sounded like footsteps. I stopped and listened.

"What are you doing?" Junchao asked, her dark eyes darting around the room.

"Nothing, Junchao. Everything's great," I said. I was sure that it had only been my own footsteps I heard.

I picked up the remote and flopped back onto the couch. "Good night, Sunny."

Sunny slid slowly off the couch. Before she had even taken a step, we heard it again.

Wooo. Wooo. Wooooo.

Alice, Junchao, and I looked at Sunny.

"There is a scientific explanation for that," she said. But I could see a lot more white in Sunny's eyes than I wanted to see right now. It made her look not so sure, and I'd never seen Sunny look not so sure about anything.

Then there was a *click*.

Followed by a *beep*.

All the lights in the house blinked off. The television flashed . . . and then went black.

18

Be the Tiger . . .
or the Antelope . . .
or the Guinea Pig

Sunny was the first to dive under the blanket, but the three of us were super close behind her.

"What are we gonna do?" Junchao's eyes were so wide that they seemed to be shouting at me when she blinked.

"Maybe I should go get Mrs. Song," I said, totally hoping someone would disagree.

Alice came through for me. "Nooo! You can't do that, Masha. She'll call my mom. And then my dad will be here in less than three minutes to take me home."

"Okay, okay," I said. "We'll figure this out. Maybe we should go turn on the lights."

"Can we stay under the blanket and all go together?" Junchao asked.

"That won't work," Alice said, pointing at her legs. Alice didn't really walk that well.

"We'll carry you," Junchao said.

"No, thanks," said Alice.

Sweat tickled my neck as it ran down into my pajamas. "Okay." I gulped. "I'll go out and turn them on."

"Do you want me to go with you?" Junchao asked. I could tell that she was totally hoping I'd say no.

"I can go faster if I'm alone," I told her, which was probably true, but who cares how fast you can go when all you're doing is running right into the clutches of a ghost.

Junchao smiled with relief.

"Tigers do everything alone," Sunny said. "Spiders do too. They're called solitary animals. This way they have more space to live in and they don't have to share their food."

20

"And why are you telling us this right now?" I asked.

"I'm giving you examples of the kinds of animals that do things alone, like you're about to do."

"But Masha isn't about to hunt antelope or spin a web to catch a fly," Alice said.

"Yeah, she's more likely to be the antelope or the fly," Junchao added.

My stomach gurgled.

"Junchao!" Alice cried. "She is not the antelope or the fly."

"Of course I didn't mean that," Junchao said. "I'm sorry, Masha. I meant you're the tiger . . . the giant, stalking, roaring, fierce tiger."

"Thanks, Junchao."

"And we'll be right here watching," Alice said.

She squeezed my hand. I squeezed hers back.

Then we slowly brought our heads out from under the cover. The cool air made my eyes sting with tears. All four of us searched the darkness . . . for a flapping white sheet, or a floating skeleton, or worst of all, a howling face with black eyes.

"Does anyone see anything?" I whispered.

No one did.

"Hey," I said, having a thought that sent a wave of happiness through me so big that it felt like Christmas morning and all the presents under the tree had my name on them. "Maybe the lights in the entire town are out and this whole thing is just a big electrical problem!"

"Yeah," said Junchao. "It's probably just a power outage. Good thinking, Masha. "

It was good thinking. But why hadn't Sunny thought of it? Then again, it's not like she's the only one who had good thoughts in this house. I had good thoughts too. Now I needed to think of a way to find out if it was a power outage.

"Stand up on the couch and look out the window. If the streetlight is off, then the town is out. If the streetlight is on, then it's just us," Sunny said.

Okay, so she had a few more good thoughts than I did.

I threw off the blanket and stood up on the couch.

22

The streetlight was on. Shoot—Christmas was over.

I dropped down and pulled the blanket back up over my shoulders.

"Anyone have any last-minute advice before I go for the lights?" I asked.

Junchao moaned.

"When you get off the couch, don't put your feet right by it," Alice said.

"Why?"

"The tiny men." She pointed down by the bottom of the couch.

"The what?" I asked.

"Tiny men. They live under things like couches and beds. My grandmother says that if you put your feet on the floor next to the bed in the night, they will pull you under and . . ."

"Stop! Don't tell me what they do," I said.

"Have you ever seen them?" asked Junchao.

"My grandmother bought me a ship captain's bed that has drawers under it, so the little men can't live under my bed. So I've never seen them."

23

I looked over the side of the couch. The moonlight coming through the window made a shadow fall on the floor, so I couldn't see whether or not there were any tiny guys hiding below.

"Put your foot down and test it," Sunny suggested, her stinky breath hot on my neck. "It's what a scientist would do."

"You put your foot down and test it. You're the scientist," I snapped.

"Haven't you ever heard of a guinea pig?" Sunny asked.

I ignored her. For some reason I was feeling like this ghost stuff was all Sunny's fault, which of course I knew that it wasn't. Anyway, just the thought of my bare foot dangling over the side of the couch made me shiver.

I looked over at the light switch by the kitchen door and wondered if I could jump from the couch all the way over to it. But that's when I had another good thought. "Wait," I said. "I don't have to run across the room. I can just turn on the lamp."

"Good idea," Junchao whispered.

24

I reached out my hand about three inches toward the lamp. I tried not to picture something grabbing me. My fingers wiggled about in the air. The lamp was still pretty far away. I needed to lean out of the blanket more.

Now my shoulder and a big chunk of my body were completely available to the ghost. But I was almost there. I felt up along the stem of the lamp in the dark to the silver key-looking thing that turned it on. I snapped it around. The light did not come on.

"Turn it again," Junchao squeaked.

I snapped it again.

Nothing.

Snap.

Nothing.

Snap.

Nothing*snap*nothing*snap*nothing . . . that is, until Junchao screamed!

All four of us met back under the blanket.

"We can't keep doing this," I huffed. "We're going to suffocate in here."

"Why is the light not working?" Alice whined.

"The ghost did it," cried Junchao.

We all crowded in closer together. None of us wanted our arms or legs out where a cold, ghostly claw could wrap around them.

"I'm sure the lightbulb just burned out," I said.

"An LED, or 'light-emitting diode,' lightbulb can last up to fifty thousand hours," said Sunny.

"That's over a year!" Junchao moaned.

"Actually it's almost six years," Sunny said.

"Well, we must have brought this lightbulb from Pennsylvania when we moved," I grumbled. "Because it just burned out." I tried to scratch my nose under the blanket and ended up elbowing Junchao in the stomach by accident. "Sorry."

"That's okay," Junchao said. "But Alice, get off my leg."

"You're on my leg," said Alice.

"I think that's me," I admitted. "Listen, I need to get to the light by the kitchen."

No one said anything.

"I'm going now," I said very bravely, but my stomach was shaking.

26

"*Xing Yun San You* forever," Alice whispered.

Junchao nodded, her hair sticking to the top of the blanket in a wild black mess. "Come back to us, Masha. Because two isn't a very lucky number."

"We'd actually be three again." Sunny shrugged, pointing at Alice, Junchao, and herself.

I growled at my little sister.

"But four is a good number too," she added. "It's the natural number that follows three and precedes five. It's also the only number that has the same number of characters as its value in the English language. You know, the word *four* has four letters. And let's not forget that it's also a highly composite number. And everybody knows that the number four is the only even number—"

"Sunny," I hissed. Maybe getting snatched away forever by a ghost wouldn't be that bad.

I peeked out from the blanket and looked all around the room one more time. There were about a billion places for a ghost to hide along the path to the light switch:

Crouched behind the green chair . . .

Under the piano bench . . .

Behind the drapes like Sunny . . .

So what I had to do was jump over the coffee table, run past the green chair and the piano bench, flip on the switch, and then run back before the ghost could get me. Sunny, Junchao, and Alice stuck their heads out from under the blanket to watch.

"Here goes," I whispered.

I stood up on the couch . . . and then I leaped over the coffee table, ran across the living room as far away from the green chair as I could, and dove by the piano bench while reaching for the switch.

I turned it on.

No light.

Junchao gave a squeaky yelp.

From the hall came the *clomp, clomp, clomp* of footsteps.

It was like all the electricity that had been sucked out of our lights was zinging through my body and making every single hair on my head stand straight up.

I couldn't think.

I couldn't move.

All I could do was flip that dumb switch up and down and up and down until . . .

Wooo. Wooo. Wooooo.

I flew back across the room and onto the couch, knocking into Sunny, Alice, and Junchao like a bowling ball into bowling pins.

There really was a ghost!

Team Smasha

We wrestled the blanket back over our heads and wrapped ourselves into a four-person ball underneath it.

"I have to get Mrs. Song," I panted.

"No!" Alice shouted right into my ear.

"I want to go home," Junchao whimpered.

"You can't," said Sunny.

"Why not?" asked Junchao.

Sunny was quiet for a second. And then she said, "Because you'd have to go out there to get home, and the ghost might get you."

"Wait a minute," I said. "I thought you said there was no such thing as ghosts."

"Well, I'm not always right, Masha."

"That's right," I said. "You're not."

Although somehow this was making her right *and* making ghosts real.

"Aren't you at least going to try to use science to explain this?" I asked. I couldn't believe that I was actually begging Sunny to be her pain-in-the-butt self.

"With average use, an LED lightbulb should last as long as twenty years, and therefore, it's improbable that it should burn out," she said. "But all the LED lightbulbs in the house burning out at exactly the same time? I would say that is impossible."

"What does that mean?"

"It means there's a ghost!" Junchao cried. "You have to wake up Mrs. Song."

"No, you can't!" Alice yelled.

"Okay, okay," I said. "Let's just think. We can deal with this, can't we?"

"Deal with a ghost?" asked Junchao.

"Yes," I said. "We just need a plan to get rid of him."

"How do you know it's a him?" asked Sunny.

Somehow, the idea of a lady ghost seemed scarier than a man ghost. I pictured her floating over the coffee table a few feet away, grinning down at the four of us clumped under our blanket, and all I wanted to do was shrink to the size of a cornbread crumb.

"Come on now, guys, think. What do we do? How do we get the ghost to go away?" I said.

"We need to exercise him," said Alice.

"You mean exorcise," said Sunny.

"That sounds too scary," said Junchao.

I didn't say anything, but I thought so too.

"Sunny, where does Mom keep the flashlight?"

"In the kitchen cabinet next to the stove," she said.

The three of us groaned. The kitchen.

"If we can grab my braces and crutches," Alice said, "we can all go together to the kitchen. My dad put them by the front door."

It was a good idea to get them, not just so that we could all get to the kitchen, but in case we needed to run away from a ghost. Can you even run away from a ghost? That question made my heart flutter in my chest. I didn't know, but I did know that we needed Alice with us. "Yes, let's get your stuff," I said.

Once again, we slowly took the blanket off our heads. Before anything else strange or scary could happen, I quickly rolled up the blanket in a ball and threw it out into the middle of the room.

"What did you do that for?" Junchao said.

"We can't keep hiding under the blanket all night. We need to get rid of this ghost." I was sounding pretty brave for someone who felt like throwing her arms up in the air and running out of the house screaming like a freak.

"How are we going to do that?" asked Junchao.

"How about we get to my room," Sunny said. "I have some science equipment that might help us. And I have Mommy's iPad. We can look up ghost removal," Sunny said.

"You're brilliant, Sunny!" Junchao said.

"Oh yes," I said. "Let's say that again because I don't think that Sunny gets to hear that enough."

"You're brilliant—"

"So this is the plan," I said, cutting Junchao off. That girl does not understand sarcasm at all, and I didn't have time to teach it to her. "Junchao and I are going to get Alice's walking equipment by the front door, and then all four of us will head to the kitchen for the flashlight, and then we'll go to Sunny's room."

"But the front door is scary," Junchao whined.

We all looked over at it.

She was right.

It was scary.

Long, stretchy shadows of tree branches flooded the floor through the front door window. On either side of the door were deep, dark corners, and anything could be hiding there. And then there was the front hall closet.

The front hall closet was scary even on a bright, sunny day. It was filled with old coats that no one ever wore, had boxes of mysterious stuff stacked on its floor, and its top shelf held my mother's collection of matryoshka dolls, which were these creepy wooden dolls with giant staring eyes and no arms or legs. Inside each doll were more dolls. Lots more. I always hated this idea, that all those other little dolls with staring eyes were sitting in the dark inside each other. And now they were all sitting in the closet . . . with the ghost.

"Where do you think ghosts live?" I asked, hoping bucketfuls of hope that no one would say closets.

"The attic," said Alice.

I sighed a giant sigh of relief.

"My grandmother once told us that my brother and I had an older sister named Elizabeth who lived in the attic. And she only came down at night. My grandmother said that Elizabeth would brush our hair and sing to us while we were asleep. But anyway, Elizabeth wasn't a ghost, so maybe that doesn't count."

"I don't ever want to meet your grandmother," I said.

I glanced back over at the door. *Ghosts live in the attic . . . with Elizabeth*, I told myself. They don't live in closets. But it's not like we have to open it. The walking stuff was sitting by the door, and not inside that closet . . . with all the creepy, staring dolls.

"We can do this, Junchao." I looked into her eyes. "Remember the bugs at summer camp? Remember how scared you were of them? But by the end of camp, you knew everything about them and were practically BFFs with anything that crept or crawled, even spiders!"

"I don't want to make friends with this ghost," she said.

"We don't have to make friends with it. We just have to get Alice's stuff so that we can get to Sunny's room and learn how to get rid of it."

"Okay, Masha," she said. "I'm with you."

But she wasn't.

As soon as we stepped off the couch onto the coffee table (to avoid the tiny men), Junchao turned around and jumped right back onto the couch with Alice and Sunny. I was right behind her.

"Why'd you do that?" I huffed, trying to catch my breath. Without the blanket, we were totally exposed.

"I thought I smelled something!" she said.

The four of us sniffed.

"Like a cinnamon bun?" asked Sunny.

"You smell cinnamon buns?" I asked.

"No," she said. "I'm just hungry."

"How can you be hungry when we might be ghost food at any second?" I whispered at her. Then I turned to Junchao. "What did you think you smelled?"

She shrugged. "I don't know. Maybe nothing." She hung her little head and all her black hair slid over her face.

I looked over at the front door. I knew that I had to go and get Alice's stuff, even if it meant going to the front door alone. I didn't smell anything, but I did hear something. It sounded like *boom, boom, boom*. It was my heart . . . beating away in my chest. "I'll be right back," I said.

"You know that's what they all say in the movies when they go off alone . . . that they'll be right back," Alice said. "And they never come back."

She was right. But Junchao wouldn't go and Alice couldn't go. I looked over at Sunny.

"I'll go," she said.

I looked into her big eyes. She didn't look afraid. "Okay," I said. "Ready?"

Sunny answered by crawling to the edge of the couch. I followed her.

"We're a team," she whispered hotly into my ear.

"Shh," I said. But then, because it was awfully nice that she volunteered to come with me, I added, "We're Munny."

Sunny giggled. "Or Smasha."

I couldn't stop myself from giggling too.

Sunny grabbed my hand, and we left the safety of the group. We stepped silently onto the top of the coffee table, and then off the other side. We stared out across the living room and then back at each other, and then we headed out into the abyss. We moved slowly, tripping over each other's feet as we made our way toward the brown chair that sat between the big picture window and the front door. Once at the brown chair, we stopped for a rest.

"You okay?" I whispered.

"Yeah," she said, smiling up at me.

Just as we were about to take another step toward the front door, we heard them . . . the *clomp, clomp, clomp* of the footsteps.

38

We grabbed onto each other and dropped to the ground. The footsteps stopped. We could hear Junchao and Alice breathing from the couch. Or at least I hoped that it was Junchao and Alice.

Then came that terrible howl.

Wooo. Wooo. Wooooo.

"Sunny!" I whispered. "Let's get those braces and crutches."

I wasn't sure if I actually said the words or just thought them—but I felt Sunny move forward. And I moved forward with her. We clung to each other so tightly that we were basically one person, half-crawling toward the front door. I didn't see Alice's stuff before I stumbled over it. I grabbed her leg braces, and Sunny picked up her crutches. We turned around, and Sunny bumped Alice's crutches into the wall. The loud thump made us freeze in place. I peeked back toward the closet door.

Was it a tiny bit open?

It was a tiny bit open!

My heart started banging in my chest.

There are no such things as ghosts.

My heart thumped away.

There is no such thing as little men that live under couches that grab your feet and pull you under.

My heart was obviously not listening to me at all.

Only mice live in attics . . . or in closets.

I looked closer into the darkness of the closet. I thought I saw the shining of two eyes.

"Sunny," I whispered.

"I hear it," she said.

"What? What do you hear?" I whisper-screeched.

"Your heart," she said. "It's tachycardic. That means that it's beating really fast. But don't worry, you can't explode your heart. It can actually beat up to two hundred times a minute for a long time and still be fine."

My heart felt like it was now beating five hundred times a minute, and I was sure that it would explode.

"Sunny," I said.

"What?"

"I think the ghost is in the coat closet."

I don't know who leaped first, but we were both back on the couch with Alice's stuff in less time than it took Junchao and Alice to yell when we crashed into them.

The four of us sat clinging to each other with Alice's braces and crutches jabbing each of us in different places. All I could think was that we had made it! Sunny and I were back on the couch alive!

Although I totally wished I hadn't thrown the blanket away.

So You Think You Have a Ghost?

Alice managed to get her braces on even with the three of us squished up next to her. I kept my eyes locked on the closet door. I couldn't totally tell, but it looked like it had opened just a tiny bit more.

We had to get to the kitchen.

"Ready?" I asked. The only response I got was Junchao's nails digging into my arm. "Maybe we should line up and—"

Before I could finish, Sunny hopped from the couch and took off.

Junchao, Alice, and I didn't even blink—we just ran—in a big ball of arms and legs and the metal of Alice's crutches. It was only about twenty feet to the kitchen, but I was panting like a dog stuck in a hot car when I got there. So were Alice and Junchao.

"Sunny!" I hissed, stopping in the center of our kitchen to breathe some more. "You could have waited."

"Sorry, I was scared," she said, turning her back to rummage around in the kitchen drawer for the flashlight.

"You don't sound scared."

She turned around with the flashlight on and shined it right in our eyes.

Junchao, Alice, and I moaned and ducked.

"Give that to me," I said, taking it from her.

I scanned the kitchen with the light. Everything looked normal. The big spaghetti pot was on the back burner of the stove, where my mom liked to keep it. The salt and pepper shakers with the big *S* and big *P* sat on the kitchen counter next to the cutting board.

The yellow clock ticked on the wall over the sink. "Boy, that clock sounds loud, doesn't it?" I whispered.

"My grandmother says that if a clock stops while you're in the room it means that you're going to die," Alice said.

"That's called predictive superstition," Sunny said. "When you believe that an event, like a clock stopping, will cause something to happen in the future."

"Would all four of us die?" asked Junchao. "Or does the clock pick one of us?"

"We have the flashlight now," I said, changing the subject. "Let's go to Sunny's room for supplies and my mom's iPad. And," I said, "can we do it without freaking out, please? We have to keep it together if we're going to get rid of this ghost. I'm going to go first. Sunny will come next. Alice will follow Sunny. And Junchao will come after Alice."

"Why do I have to go last?" Junchao whined.

"Because you are the bravest," I said.

Junchao gave her famous ho-ho-ho laugh. It's the first time she did that since we discovered we had a

44

ghost. It made me feel like maybe we could fix this . . . if we stuck together.

We lined up in our order and headed out of the kitchen and down the hall toward Sunny's room. It was the first door on the left down the hall, so we didn't have far to walk. Although it *was* far enough for Sunny to practically pull my pajama pants off me. I had to hold them up with one hand and shine the white beam of light with the other.

For one second, I thought about going straight down the hall into my mother's room, where I knew Mrs. Song was sleeping. She would know what to do about the ghost in our front hall closet. Mrs. Song knew a lot about stuff that you wouldn't think she knew. Like she knew how to play the flute. And she knew all about starfish.

But I couldn't do it to Alice. She was right. Her parents would never let her go to another sleepover again.

It was just one ghost.

We could get rid of one ghost.

And maybe we were wrong to be scared of it. Maybe it was one of those nice ghosts, you know, the

45

kind that are just stuck here and really want to move on. Maybe it needed our help. Maybe we would help it and then we'd actually be sad when it left. Maybe it would even tell us some great secret, like where a treasure was hidden, or . . .

There was a crashing sound like someone banging cymbals together.

Our orderly little line scattered as if we were ants whose rock had just been turned over. We piled into Sunny's room. Junchao and I dragged Alice under her armpits straight from the door to Sunny's bed—with all of us yanking our bare feet up and away from the little men underneath it.

Alice grabbed Sunny's pillows and piled them up in front of us like a giant fluffy wall. When I saw what she was doing, I scooped up Sunny's stuffed animals and made them part of the wall too. A bunch of stuffing between us and the ghost was better than *not* having a bunch of stuffing between us and the ghost.

Once we were done, the four of us peered out over the fluffy barricade at Sunny's open door . . . waiting. Would the ghost walk right in or float in like you see on TV? Would it be carrying cymbals or was it able to make different sounds using only its ghost mind?

There was a *plunk, plunk, plunk* sound at the window, followed by lots more *plunks*. It was raining. "Maybe that crash was just thunder," I said.

A giant flash of lightning lit up the room . . . followed by the biggest clap of thunder I'd ever heard.

"Why is there a storm?" Junchao moaned.

"Because strong rising warm air currents called updrafts are meeting with cooler downdrafts," said Sunny.

"I know that," said Junchao. "But why now? Don't you think it's weird?"

"There are an estimated forty-four thousand thunderstorms that occur around the Earth every day," Sunny added. "So this is not much of a coincidence."

"My grandmother says that spirits take energy from things around them," Alice said. "And a storm has electricity in it, right, Sunny? And that's energy."

I looked over at my little sister. Lightning lit up her face. Thunder rumbled. It was so loud that it seemed to shake the room. But maybe it was just me that was shaking.

"Yes, thunderstorms have electricity in them. And electricity is energy."

"So the ghost is getting lots of energy from this storm," Alice whispered.

Junchao squished down deeper between the wall and the pillows. "I don't like the idea of an energetic ghost."

Another bolt of lightning flashed. All four of us held on to one another as we waited for the crash of the thunder. We still jumped when it hit.

"Where is the iPad, Sunny?"

"Over on my desk," she said.

Sunny's desk was pushed up under the window at the end of her bed. I squinted over at it in the dark. It was overflowing with papers, wires, and metal junk, and there were a million jars and glass beakers filled with weird stuff floating in them.

"Go get it," I said.

"Not me," she squealed.

"You weren't scared when you ran into the kitchen."

48

"I was too. That's why I ran."

My heart fell. I didn't want to have to go over there.

I shined the light around her desk.

We screamed! *There in my beam of light was the ghost.*

Or . . . maybe not the ghost . . . but something absolutely horrible.

"That's just Allan," Sunny said. "He's an anatomical model."

"He's a skeleton!" Junchao shouted. She was halfway under the pillow wall and shaking as if she were wearing a wet bathing suit at the North Pole.

"It's okay," I told her. "It's just some of Sunny's science junk." But I felt a little like my neck was going to let my head roll right off of it. Being scared was a lot of work.

"Listen, Sunny," I said. "Since you're the one who is best friends with the skeleton . . ."

"Allan," she said.

"You really are a mad scientist," I growled.

"Mad sounds too emotional," Sunny said, smiling like I'd just complimented her. "I would say that I'm a different kind of sane."

49

"Well then, take your different kind of sane self over to your desk and get the iPad."

"What about the little men under the bed?" she whined.

Junchao gave a howl and burrowed even deeper under our pillow wall. She was practically part of the wall now. "Did you see the little men?" Her voice was muffled by Sunny's brown teddy bear. "Do you think they can climb up to the top of the bed?"

"No one saw any little men," I said. "And no, they cannot climb." But I quickly sucked in a big breath and held it as I glanced down at Sunny's pink comforter—my heart thumping as I waited to see if teeny monster guys were clinging to the ruffles and making their way up to us.

Nothing moved.

I let out all the air in me in one long breath.

Then I glared at Alice.

She shrugged. "It was my grandmother, not me," she whispered.

"How about I shine the light and you run go get the iPad," Sunny said.

I tried to think of a way out of this, but only for a second because I knew I was going to have to go get it.

I scanned the room with the flashlight, making sure to recheck the edge of the bed for any monster men peering up at me. No little eyes. I kept the light away from Sunny's bony little best friend. Fortunately, I could see my mom's iPad sitting on top of one of Sunny's books on the desk toward the back. Unfortunately, I could also see all of Sunny's creepy science stuff.

"What is that floating in the pickle jar next to the iPad?" I asked.

"That's a specimen jar, not a pickle jar," said Sunny.

"What is the thing in the *specimen* jar," I demanded.

Junchao crawled out from under the pillows and peeked over at the desk. "Oh my gosh!" she shouted. "It's a human brain."

All three of us gasped.

"Whose brain is it?" Alice asked.

"Don't tell us!" I said. "We don't need to know."

Maybe my little sister was really and truly mad. Maybe she was doing horrible things to more people

than just me. Maybe she was going to do that to *my* brain one day!

I looked down at Sunny. She smiled back at me. I shivered.

"It's not a human brain." She giggled.

I felt myself relax. Of course it wasn't a human brain. It was probably just a piece of floating clay made to look like a brain. Maybe it even doubled as a pencil sharpener. My mom had a statue of a little puppy on her desk that was also a pencil sharpener. She'd always wanted a dog, but Sunny is allergic to their hair.

"It's a cow's stomach," Sunny said. "The butcher at the ShopRite saved it for me."

"Yuck!" Alice said.

"Does Mommy you know you have that?" I demanded.

"She asked the butcher for me," she said.

"That is disgusting, Sunny," I said.

"Well, I'm not the one who eats cows, Masha. That would be you." She chuckled.

"You just stuff their stomachs in jars!"

Before Sunny could say anything, we heard them.

CLOMP. CLOMP. CLOMP.

They sounded closer than they ever had before.

We all dropped down behind the pillow wall.

I held my head stiff and still so I could hear as well as possible. The rain beat against the window, but the thunder and lightning had quieted down. I didn't hear the ghost. Was it floating right outside in the hall? Was it thinking about coming in?

Wooo. Wooo. Wooooo.

We all jumped, clanking our heads together as we dove under the pillows.

"We need that iPad," Sunny whispered.

She was right. She was always right.

I took a big breath and sat up. Alice and Sunny did too. Junchao didn't.

I looked around the room with the flashlight. Nothing. I pointed the light back on Sunny's desk, trying not to look too closely at the cow guts in the jar or the stupid skeleton. And then I told myself to move . . . but I didn't.

"What are you doing?" Alice said.

"Getting ready."

"You know that I'd do it if I could. Right, Masha?" she said.

I looked over at my friend. She gave me that curvy smile that I love. "I know you would." Alice made me want to be brave. She always did.

"You know that I *can't* do it. Right, Masha?" Junchao whimpered from under the pillow.

"You're always my *gui mi,* no matter what you can or can't do," I told her.

I heard a muffled "ho-ho-ho" coming from under the pillow.

When Sunny glued plastic flowers to my head and I had to shave all my hair off and no one would talk to me at school, Junchao told me I looked cool. She was super brave when it came to standing up to people, just not ghosts. But people can sometimes be scarier than ghosts.

I breathed.

And then I jumped.

I barely felt Sunny's rug under my bare feet before I was at the desk. I reached across it.

Lightning blinded me.

I knocked over a beaker.

"Watch out! That's my density experiment!" Sunny shout-whispered, making me lose my balance.

I reached out to break my fall. I grabbed a hold of something thin and smooth . . . and not at all strong enough to stop me from falling. I think it was a rib. Whatever it was, it cracked right off in my hand and I landed in a tangled heap on top of Sunny's skeleton.

"ALLAN!"

My pajamas got hooked onto a couple of bony fingers. I tried to get away, but he held on to me tightly.

Thunder shook the room.

I ripped the bones from my pants and threw that thing about ten feet. It sounded like a thousand pots falling when it hit the wall.

I was so out of there.

I leaped off the ground as if it were on fire, swiped the iPad off the desk, and swiveled around toward the bed just in time for the flashlight to go out.

"Help!"

I hopped across the room like a crazy rabbit, lifting my feet up high so each of them was spending as little time as possible on the floor. Two steps from safety, something touched my toe. It felt just like a tiny hand!

I flung myself at the bed, ramming into Alice.

She hugged me tight.

I was safe . . . I was safe . . . I was safe.

My heart thudded in my ears.

I was safe . . . I was safe . . . I was safe.

I never wanted her to let me go—except that I did—because she was hugging me so hard that I was sure she would crack my mom's iPad, and I really needed her to let go of my lungs so I could breathe.

"Allan," Sunny moaned.

"The battery died!" I howled as soon as I had enough air in my lungs so I wouldn't die.

"Highly unlikely," Sunny whispered.

I would have strangled her, but my arms felt like wet noodles after being almost eaten by the little men. "Just find out how to get rid of the ghost," I told her, handing her the iPad.

56

She turned it on and began to search. "Okay," she said, her face lit up by the glow of the screen. "This looks like a good site. It's called UnwantedGhost dot com."

"That sounds perfect," Alice said.

Junchao unburied herself from our wall of pillows and stuffed animals.

Sunny read, "'So you think you have a ghost? The first thing you will want to do is keep from jumping to conclusions. You must make sure that you have a real ghost. Many times there can be a logical explanation for strange occurrences in your home. Just because a door rattles or you hear a bang in the basement is not proof that you have a ghost in your house.'"

"It sounds reasonable," Junchao said.

I agreed. It did sound reasonable. Maybe we were jumping to conclusions. Had I really seen a ghost in the closet? Did the door really open up wider after Sunny and I got back to the couch? Could it just be Mrs. Song walking around in her sleep and snoring in a strange, ghost-howling way? *This whole thing was probably a mistake.*

Sunny continued, "'Perhaps you are feeling drafts. Many old homes don't have enough insulation and may even have cracks in their walls where air is getting in. Just by fixing these cracks, you may notice that the drafts are gone and that the door that seemed to open or close all on its own has stopped.'"

I bet this was it! A draft opened the front hall closet. It wasn't a ghost. I could feel Alice and Junchao relaxing a little too as we listened to Sunny.

"'If lights in your home turn on and off, you should have your electrical system checked right away. It is most likely faulty or damaged wiring and not a ghost.'"

Of course! Of course it's faulty wiring. Happiness filled my chest. My stomach growled. I was hungry. I thought about the rest of Mrs. Song's dumplings in the kitchen. We could heat those up and then watch a movie . . . not a scary movie, just a movie. And thank goodness I did not wake up Mrs. Song!

Sunny kept reading.

"'Have you heard knocking or tapping on your walls? You may have something living in your walls, but that something isn't necessarily a ghost. It's most likely a rodent. It may also be a tree branch scraping against the outside walls of your house. Check your basement and attic for critters such as mice, raccoons, squirrels, or bats. Check your exterior walls for branches or anything that might be swinging in the wind and bumping against your home.'"

A raccoon! That's what the footsteps were. It wasn't Mrs. Song but a raccoon. It was probably walking around on the roof. Or maybe it got into the attic. Raccoons are so cute, but still, they shouldn't be in your house.

I'd tell my mom as soon as she got home tomorrow. And I'd tell her that she had to call an electrician too. Mrs. Song's son was an electrician. And he was really nice. He always gave Sunny and me little toys out of his truck when he visited Mrs. Song. Last time he gave us these little plastic soldier guys with parachutes stuck to them. Sunny and I had so much fun winding up the parachutes into balls around the soldiers, throwing them out of Mrs. Song's second-floor bathroom window, and watching them float down into her azalea bushes.

The raccoon that is up in the attic probably ate through some wires up there and now our lights are out. All I had to do was tell my mom all about it when she got home. I wondered what Mrs. Song's son would bring Sunny and me this time.

My stomach grumbled again. *Mrs. Song's dumplings, here we come!*

Sunny was still reading.

I tried to pay attention even though all I wanted to do was think about dumplings in salty soy sauce.

"'Once you have reviewed any maintenance or repairs that your house may need, only then can you consider that you may have a ghost problem.'"

"Okay," I said. "I'll tell Mom about the raccoon and the house repairs when she gets home tomorrow. So do you guys want to go eat more dumplings?"

"What raccoon?" asked Junchao.

"I'm not done," Sunny said. "I didn't get to the ten warning signs."

"Warning signs?" I asked.

60

Sunny read, "'Below are the ten warning signs to determine if there is ghostly activity in your home. If you have experienced any of these ten warning signs, or more than one, you may not be alone in your home.'"

"I don't like the sound of that," said Junchao.

I didn't either.

Warning Signs

Warning signs,'" read Sunny. "'Number one: Items in your home disappear, then reappear frequently.'"

Alice and Junchao looked at me. "Nothing is missing," I said, kind of excited.

"What about Mommy's glasses when she was packing up for her conference?" Sunny said.

"She loses those all the time."

Sunny shrugged.

I heard Junchao gulp.

"What's the second one?" I asked.

"'Items or furniture move all on their own,'" read Sunny.

"We're good on that one," I said. "Nothing has moved. Next one!"

"'Number three: You see flashes of light.'"

"No flashes," I said.

Sunny went to open her mouth.

"That was lightning."

She shut it.

"What's the next one?" asked Junchao.

"'You see shadows moving,'" read Sunny.

Junchao, Alice, and I glanced around the room.

"No shadows," I whispered, hoping that the ghost didn't hear me and make a shadow. "So far, so good." I said. "That's four. Only six more to go."

"'Number five: You feel cold spots in your home,'" Sunny read.

"I was feeling cold before, remember?" said Alice.

"But that was the vein thing, right, Sunny?" I looked at my little sister.

She gave a tiny shrug. "I thought it was."

"Wait a minute," I said, glaring at Sunny. "What are you up to?"

"What?" asked Sunny.

"What do you mean, you *thought*. You never just *think* anything. You *know*."

"No one can know everything," she said.

I hopped to my knees on the bed. "Sunny Sweet," I said, "you are totally up to something!" How could I have not seen this before? I looked over at Alice and Junchao. Their eyes were wide as they blinked back at me in the dark. "She's behind this. Don't you see it? Don't you believe me?" I said to my friends.

"How could Sunny have made those footstep sounds or howled?" asked Alice. "She was with us."

"And she did try to be a ghost. Remember how she hid behind the curtain," Junchao added. "Plus, she doesn't even believe in ghosts."

I narrowed my eyes and frowned at my little sister.

"It says here on the site," Sunny continued, "'When we are emotionally stressed out, we attract negative energy to us.'"

"What do you mean?" I growled.

64

"I know what it means," said Alice. "My grandmother talks about it all the time. If you only look at the bad things, then sometimes the bad things find you!"

"So you think this ghost is here because I'm not being nice to my sister!" I shouted.

CLOMP. CLOMP. CLOMP.

We all dove under the pillow wall.

"That doesn't mean anything." My voice sounded really loud in my own ears under the pillows.

"Well, you did kind of yell at her to go to bed before the movie," came Junchao's muffled voice through the pillow.

"And you aren't that happy with her now, even though she's helping us," Alice added.

I couldn't believe it! My friends were joining in with my little sister against me! "So the ghost is all my fault?" My own hot breath was making my face sweat. I was just about to unbury myself from the pillows and stomp right out of Sunny's room when . . .

Wooo. Wooo. Wooooo.

Oh no. This ghost was all my fault!

All four of us squished closer together behind our pillow wall.

"Okay," I said. "Maybe I was a little too forceful about wanting Sunny to go to bed. But you guys have to admit that she wasn't listening to me and this is my sleepover."

"That's a little negative, don't you think?" said Sunny.

I lunged at her.

Junchao and Alice pounced on top of me, holding me back.

"I hate to point this out, but attacking me is also negative," Sunny said, hiding a smile.

"You don't hate pointing it out," I said, struggling to break free from my friends. "You love pointing it out!"

"Masha," Junchao said, "she's right."

How many times in my life had I heard that statement? One trillion billion times. That's how many! I broke free from Junchao and Alice, but instead of strangling Sunny, I just growled at her.

"Growling . . . ," Sunny started. Junchao covered Sunny's mouth with both her hands.

66

"It's okay, Masha," Alice said. "We don't care that you brought out the ghost. You're our friend, and we're going to help you get rid of it. Right, Junchao?"

"That's right," Junchao said. "We're all in this together." She took her hands off Sunny's mouth.

"Yes," Sunny said. "We're all in this together."

I wanted to say that I didn't bring the ghost. And that maybe it had been Sunny. Or that maybe the ghost had always been here. But I didn't like the sound of that last idea, and the one before it was probably another negative thing.

Plus, I loved my friends. They were the best friends ever not to abandon me just because I had an angry ghost following me around. But since I still didn't trust myself not to say something mega negative about puny Dr. Paranormal, I just said, "Read the next one."

"'Number six: You smell things,'" she read.

"Smell things?" I said. "Like pancakes or something?"

"No," Junchao said. "Like burned rubber."

"What do you mean?" asked Alice.

67

"Remember when I said I smelled something?" Junchao grimaced. She looked a little like she'd just shoved a big spoonful of cold lima beans in her mouth. "It was burned rubber. You know, like a car tire was burning. But you guys didn't smell it. Remember?" She looked a little hopeful.

"I smelled it," said Sunny.

I looked at Sunny . . . trying to tell if she really had smelled it. "Did you, Alice?" I asked.

"I . . . I don't . . . maybe I did. I can't remember," Alice stammered. "Does burning rubber smell a little like a hot curling iron? My mom is always curling her hair with a curling iron, and I might have smelled something like that."

"I think it does," Junchao said glumly.

"I didn't smell a curling iron," I said. "And I didn't smell any car tires either." But I could tell no one was listening to me, and I could tell that number six was already checked yes by Junchao, Alice, and Sunny.

"Listen," I said. "There was no moving furniture and no shadows and no flashing lights for sure. And cold spots and disappearing items were only kind-ofs.

So really, smelling stuff is only one definite warning sign. And one definite warning sign doesn't mean we have a ghost. Right?" I looked at Sunny. "Right, Sunny? That's only one thing so far."

Sunny looked down at the iPad screen and reread, "'If you experience any of these ten incidents, especially more than one, this is good evidence to support that you may not be alone in your home.'"

"Okay," I said. "No one panic." Unfortunately, it looked like Junchao wasn't going to listen to me. Her eyes were rolling around in her head, and she was chewing on two fingernails at once. "This is only one. And they said more than one, so we're good."

"It does say, *especially more than one*," Sunny piped in.

"See." I looked at Junchao. "Sunny agrees."

"Well, we still have four left to read," Sunny said. "But it's good that you're being positive now, Masha."

I sucked in a big breath of air instead of bopping the spawn of the devil right in the head. "Just read the next one," I said in a high-pitched voice that I hoped sounded positive.

69

"'Number seven,'" she read. "'Have you seen an apparition?'"

"What's an apparition?" asked Alice. She looked at me. I knew she knew what it was and was just hoping that this wasn't the answer.

"An apparition is the ghost," Junchao said. "Did we see the ghost?" Now Sunny looked at me. "Masha?" she asked. "Did you see it in the closet?"

I shook my head.

"You said that you saw it," Alice said.

"No I didn't." I pulled at the neck of my pajamas. It felt a little tight.

"Yes you did," Junchao said.

"Did I?" My forehead felt sweaty.

"You did," said Sunny.

"No I didn't," I insisted.

I thought about the closet door and how it was opened up just a bit. It had felt like someone was watching me. But the truth was, I didn't really *see* anything. I really didn't. *I didn't see anything!* Then my heart felt like birds were singing inside of it. I hadn't really seen anything!

"NO!" I shouted.

Everyone shushed me.

"No," I whispered. "I didn't see anything."

That was the truth. And now we were another warning sign closer to not having a ghost.

Everyone stared at me in the dark. I couldn't tell if they believed me or not. But then Sunny read number eight. "'Do you feel like you're being watched?'"

My heart fell so deep into my stomach that I swear I heard the thump of it landing. Sunny looked up from the iPad. "Does anybody feel like someone is watching us?"

I kept my mouth shut. Maybe no one had been watching us from the front hall closet. Maybe it was my mom's umbrella with the big, curvy handle that looked like it was peeking out at me. Or maybe it was just Sunny's rain boots. They have duck faces on them, and I bet it was those duck eyes that I felt staring out of the closet.

All four of us looked around the room. Sunny's closet was closed, thank goodness. But there were plenty of dark places in Sunny's room that could be hiding a spying ghost.

Under her desk, for one.

Or in Sunny's laundry basket. A ghost could totally be in there watching us from underneath Sunny's dirty underwear. Although that would be kind of gross.

"I don't think anyone is watching us," Alice whispered. "What about you guys?"

Sunny gave a little shrug, and Junchao mumbled that she didn't think so. I joined in on the end of her mumble. We were almost safe. There were only two more warning signs left. "What's the next one, Sunny?" I said, trying not to sound too pushy.

"'Number nine: Do you sometimes hear footsteps?'"

Junchao let out a little gasp, and Alice grabbed my arm.

We were done for.

"Wait, you guys. That's only two warning signs," I said.

"But the site says 'especially more than one,'" Junchao moaned.

"Yes, true, but it also says something about good evidence. Read it again, Sunny."

Sunny read it again. "'If you experience any of these ten incidents, especially more than one, this is good evidence to support that you may not be alone in your home.'"

"Oh, oh, oh," Junchao cried.

"Hold on. It says this is good evidence. It doesn't say that it's great evidence. And good isn't great." I looked over at Sunny. "Right?" I asked. "Good isn't great."

Sunny agreed that good wasn't great.

"Read the last one. We still have one more."

Sunny read it. "'Number ten: Do your lights flicker on and off?'" She looked up at us with a gasp.

Junchao gave a howl and dove under our pillow wall.

Alice and I grabbed hold of each other.

We were not alone in our home!

Ridding Your House of Unwanted Spirits: Just Ask Nicely

So we had a ghost . . .

And it was all my fault . . .

Because I'd been mean to Sunny.

This was supposed to be the most fun night of my entire life. But instead of talking about how cute Michael Capezzi was and eating way too many microwave pizza bites and trying to get Junchao to laugh her crazy Santa Claus laugh, we were stuck on Sunny's bed hiding from an evil spirit.

"What should we do?" I asked. I was kind of hoping that someone would suggest getting Mrs. Song.

It wasn't like I wanted my best friend to never see another sleepover as long as she lived, but I also didn't want a ghost to get us.

"We should call the police." Junchao's voice was muffled by all the pillows on top of her.

"The police?" I said. I pictured my mother's cell phone ringing in her conference hotel room. I pictured her sleepy face saying hello. And then I pictured her jumping up out of bed when she heard it was the police calling her from *our house*. "We are so NOT calling the police!" I said.

"Okay," said Junchao, still not coming out from under the pillow wall. "Then we have to at least wake up Mrs. Song. Maybe she won't have to call your mom, Alice."

Alice moaned. "You said that we were all in this together. If you wake up Mrs. Song then she will definitely call my mom, and I won't ever be in *anything* again."

"But then what should we do?" I whined.

"'What you should do,'" Sunny read from the website.

Junchao popped her head out from under the wall.

Alice and I looked at each other and then down at Sunny.

"Does it really say that?" I asked.

Sunny nodded her little head.

"Read it," I commanded. The three of us held our breath as Sunny read.

"'First of all, do not panic. You do have some control over these situations, and in many cases you can rid these spirits from your home.'"

"Many cases," Junchao said. "Many is just most of them. It's not all of them."

"But most is a good thing," I said.

"But not a great thing," noted Sunny.

I ignored her.

"Well, we're not panicking, right?" I asked.

Junchao and Alice stared at me.

"Right?" I repeated.

My friends mumbled "right," but not with much enthusiasm.

"You can do better than that," I said, sounding very much like my science teacher, Mrs. Hull, when no one would come forward to try to answer one of her questions.

Junchao and Alice mumbled "right" again in the exact same dull way.

I huffed. Maybe there was more to being a teacher than getting to use your cell phone when you wanted and being able to drink soda and stuff during class.

Sunny read on, "'Some ghosts can be pretty moody, and others, just plain irritable and bad-tempered, although in most instances ghosts want to get your attention and let you know that they are there. They thrive on your responses and emotions. Sometimes simply ignoring them will send them on their way.'"

"I like that," I said. "That sounds easy. Let's ignore it."

A flash of lightning blinded me. And before I could blink the light out of my eyes, thunder slammed the room. The four of us clocked heads as we grabbed each other. "Okay!" I yelled out to the ghost. "We won't ignore you."

Light thunder rumbled in the distance . . . It was as if the ghost were saying "okay."

"Masha, this is too scary," Junchao whispered into my ear.

My stomach ached. I thought so too.

We held on to each other. No lightning. No thunder. Finally we let go and I looked over at Alice. I could see that she was feeling as freaked out as Junchao but wasn't going to say it.

Sunny continued her research. "This is good, Masha. It says here on the site that when you feel or see their presence, you need to address them."

"What do you mean, address them?"

"It says you should speak to them, but only to explain politely that you would appreciate it if they would leave. It says to be loving because you don't want to get them angry or they might stay around. It says that often this will do the trick and that the ghost will leave."

"Wow," said Alice. "That sounds so easy. Go ahead, Masha, ask it to go."

"Nicely," added Junchao.

"Why do I have to do it?" I whispered so the ghost couldn't hear me.

78

"It was your negative energy that brought it," Sunny said.

I rolled my eyes.

"That's negative," Sunny said.

I growled.

"Masha," Junchao and Alice said together.

"All right," I snapped. Being nice to Sunny was just about impossible.

I turned and faced the room. I didn't know where the ghost was. I figured that if I were a ghost, I'd probably be under the desk in the corner. It was a really dark place and no one would step on you or anything if they didn't know you were there.

"Hi," I said. And I gave the ghost the peace sign.

"Don't do that," Sunny said. "The ghost might be French, and to the French that sign doesn't mean good things."

"What?" Alice said.

"Don't get her started . . . ," I said, but it was too late.

"Some people claim that the two-fingered V sign came about during the Hundred Years' War between the French and the English. The French would cut off the two arrow-shooting fingers of captured English archers so they couldn't fire an arrow at them ever again. The English took to holding up two fingers to the French as a sign of defiance. In other words, they were saying to the French that they still had two fingers and could shoot them."

"In other words," I said, "shh!" And then, because I was supposed to be nice to Sunny, I patted her sweetly on the head.

"Ouch," she said.

Then I turned back to the ghost.

"Uh, I was wondering if you'd mind . . . well, if you wouldn't mind leaving. It's not that we don't like you. Because we don't really even know you. I'm sure if we knew you, you know, when you were alive . . . not that you're dead or anything. I mean, I don't know exactly what you are."

This wasn't going great. It wasn't even going good.

"I'm sure that whatever you are, it's something nice. I bet it's something very, very nice."

"Super nice," Sunny added.

"Yes," I said. "Super nice."

"Super-duper nice," Sunny said.

"Of course. Super-duper nice."

"Super-di-duper nice," said Sunny.

I leaped at Sunny's throat.

Alice tried to hold me back, but I was all over my little sister.

The lights in Sunny's room flashed on and then off again. And I froze, mid-strangle.

"Masha," Junchao whispered. "You're being mega negative."

"She started it," I hissed.

Sunny's three-way radio blasted on.

None of us moved. The scratchy garble on the radio was so loud that it seemed to be playing inside my head.

But then Sunny reached over and snapped it off.

The silence sizzled in my ears.

"I think you made it angry," Sunny said.

The Story of
Trudy Day

M aybe it was already angry," I said angrily.

"A lot of ghosts are," said Alice. "My grandmother says that this town has its very own ghost and that she is really angry."

"Why?" asked Junchao. Her eyes scanned the room. And I couldn't stop mine from doing the same.

"Her name was Trudy Day, and she lived here a long time ago."

"Where?" Junchao shivered and rubbed her arms with her hands.

"I don't know. My grandmother never said where. She just said that she was supposed to be majorly beautiful and that all the boys kept asking her out. But she never went out with any of them. She was saving all her love for her one true soul mate."

"What's a soul mate?" I asked.

"There is no such thing as a soul mate," Sunny said.

"You said that about ghosts," I snapped. "And look at us now."

"Anyway, there is too such a thing," Alice insisted. "My grandmother says that everyone has one. Your soul mate is the one person in the world that gets you more than any other."

I thought about Michael Capezzi and wondered if he was my soul mate.

"And Trudy Day was waiting for hers to come," continued Alice. "Then one day, this really cute guy came to town. Trudy and this guy went out a few times. He took her on long walks. He wrote her love letters. They held hands. Trudy fell totally in love and believed that this guy was her soul mate."

"Was he?" asked Junchao.

Alice shook her head no. I didn't like where this story was going.

"One day, the guy brought her a beautiful red rose. He said that she was prettier than anything in the world, including the rose. But he told her that he didn't love her and that he was going away."

"Oh no." Junchao sighed.

"Trudy got so mad. I mean, my grandmother said that Trudy got madder than anybody else has ever been mad before. And that her anger built up and up and up, until it became a monster that tracked down that guy and killed him."

"What?" I said. "Anger can do that?" I glanced over at Sunny. My anger at my little sister got pretty big sometimes.

"Trudy couldn't control her anger. It had a mind of its own. And it boomeranged right back at Trudy and killed her too!"

"Wow," I breathed. "People should learn how to not get so mad." I felt a little sweaty under my arms.

84

"And this is the worst part," Alice continued.

"There is a worse part?" squeaked Junchao.

"My grandmother says that the day after Trudy died, guess who came into town looking for her?"

"Her real soul mate!" Junchao yelled.

"That's right. And so Trudy rose from the dead to be with him. But of course she couldn't because she was dead. And so her ghost haunts anyone in town who is filled with love."

"Oh no," Junchao cried. "I'm filled with love!"

"You are filled with love," Alice said, patting Junchao on the arm. "But I think Trudy haunts people who are *in* love."

"Well then, our ghost isn't Trudy because no one here is in love," I said.

"You like that boy Michael," Junchao pointed out.

"But I don't love him," I grumbled.

"Are you sure?" Sunny asked.

"Wait a minute," I said. "How can our ghost be here because of my negative energy *and* because I think Michael Capezzi is kind of cute?"

"Maybe both things brought Trudy," Sunny said.

85

"I thought you didn't believe in ghosts. And I thought you didn't believe in soul mates. And now you believe in both?" I snapped.

"You're being negative," Junchao whispered.

I looked over at Alice for help. She squinted her eyes and gave me a little shrug.

I let my head fall back on my neck. Trudy was haunting me for just liking a boy? I'd never even held his hand! It didn't seem very fair.

Ridding Your House of Unwanted Spirits: Dress for It

How do we save Masha?" Junchao moaned.

I wished that I could just crawl under the bed and forget about this whole night . . . except that now I knew there were little men under there that wanted to eat me.

Alice hugged me. "It's okay, Masha. We're going to fix this."

"How?" I asked.

"We have to get the ghost out, that's all," Alice said. "We'll make her go. The first thing we should do is light lots and lots of candles. My grandmother says that candles keep ghosts out of your house."

"We aren't allowed to light candles," I said.

"Also," added Sunny. "Trudy is already in the house." She looked at me and gave me a little smile that said: *because of you*.

"Don't call her that." I scowled. It was so hard not to be negative with dinky Dr. Evil reminding me how this whole thing was my fault.

"What about garlic? We can string garlic all around like Christmas lights," said Alice.

"Isn't that to keep vampires away?" I asked.

"Vampires," Junchao whispered as she chewed on a long strand of her hair and searched the room with her eyes.

Sunny gave a little sigh and then jumped off the bed and headed to her closet.

"Sunny!"

I know that I often wanted to kill my little sister, but I didn't want her to *be* killed.

88

"The ghost isn't in here anymore," she said. "The thermometer on the iPad shows that the temperature has increased in the room. That means she's gone."

I shivered. *She was in here?*

Sunny opened up her closet, fished around a bunch in the dark, and then pulled out new batteries.

"You're a genius," Alice said.

I coughed.

Junchao and Alice looked over at me.

"My throat's a little dry," I said.

Sunny put batteries into the flashlight and turned it on. Light filled the room. We all took a big breath and relaxed . . . a little.

Then Sunny turned back to her closet and started pulling down hangers and taking off the clothes. "If we're going after Trudy, we need to protect ourselves," she said.

"Really, stop calling her that," I said.

Sunny handed us each a wire hanger. "We need to put these on our heads. UnwantedGhost dot com said that ghosts don't like metal. Now, I know what you're thinking—that these hangers are made out of steel, which is technically not a metal. But steel is an alloy of iron, and iron is a metal."

Something a ghost didn't *technically* like was good enough for us. Alice, Junchao, and I quickly twisted our hangers into a shape that would stay on our heads.

"Also, we need to attach these to the hangers," Sunny said, handing us pencils. "The pencils are yellow. And the color yellow is used in the ancient Chinese system called *feng shui* to help create positive energy."

Alice and I looked at Junchao to see if it was true.

"Why are you staring at me?" Junchao frowned. "Just because I'm part Chinese doesn't mean I know a thousand years' worth of Chinese history."

"It's closer to four thousand years," Sunny said. "The first written history in China is recorded at around 1700 BC." She went on about some sort of dynasty as she got the tape from her desk, but we weren't listening. We were busy taping as many pencils to the hangers as we could. When I was done with mine, I made a hanger hat for Sunny while she gathered up a bunch of equipment from her desk drawers.

"Look at mine," Junchao said, smiling and holding out her hanger hat. She had staggered her pencils so that there was a short one, and a long one, and then a short one, all the way around it.

"It looks like the crown of a king." Alice laughed. "Do you like mine?" Alice held hers up. She had taped all her pencils to the hanger only in the back.

"Yours looks like an American Indian headdress," I said. Alice smiled a giant curvy smile.

Then they both looked at the hats I'd made. The pencils weren't even at all or in any kind of pattern, but were sticking out everywhere. And there was so much tape that it looked like the pencils had gotten into a big fight with the tape, and the tape had won.

When Junchao and Alice didn't have anything to say about my hats, I started to giggle.

And then my friends started to giggle.

CLOMP. CLOMP. CLOMP.

No more giggling.

"We need to get to the bathroom," Sunny said.

"What about the ghost?" asked Junchao. "Maybe she's in the bathroom."

"I don't think ghosts like to hang out in bathrooms," Sunny said.

Wooo. Wooo. Wooooo.

The four of us quickly put on our hanger hats.

"Now we're protected." Sunny pointed at her hanger hat.

Junchao did not look convinced. But the four of us—hangers on our head and with a backpack full of Sunny's science stuff—lined up at the door. The bathroom was right across the hall from Sunny's bedroom, so we only had to make it across about three feet of rug.

I put my hand on the door handle.

"Ready?" I whispered.

Sunny might be in charge of information, but I was in charge of everything else. The three of them stood behind me, surrounding Alice on her crutches, their faces yellow in the glow of the flashlight.

They nodded their heads.

I opened the door.

My heart was quietly thumping as I stuck my head a tiny, tiny bit through the door and peeked up and down the hall.

Nothing.

I listened hard.

All I could hear was the ticking of the rain still coming down outside. I motioned that we were good to go, and then I swung open the door and jumped the three feet across the hall and into the bathroom. My bare feet hit the tile, and then Junchao, Alice, and Sunny all hit me. Alice's crutches were so light that they flew over my head and hit the toilet with a clang.

I scrambled out from under them and shut the bathroom door behind us.

"Shh!"

We were so loud that we were going to end up waking Mrs. Song for sure, and then Sunny and I would be left with a ghost and Alice would be on her way home.

I looked in the mirror to fix my hanger hat, and that's when I noticed the shower curtain behind us. It was pulled across the bathtub.

Anything could be in there.

I turned to face the curtain. Everyone looked at me looking at it. And then they all turned to face the shower curtain.

"Do it," Alice whispered.

I squinted my eyes and reached up and grabbed the shower curtain, pulling it open with a *CHHHHHHH*.

Junchao screamed.

I grabbed her mouth with both my hands and Alice grabbed me.

Sunny shined the flashlight into the bathtub.

It was empty.

We slumped onto the bathroom floor, panting.

"Why are we in here?" I asked. I should have probably asked this before we traveled across the hall.

"It says that the first step in any ghost hunt is to use the bathroom," Sunny said.

"Sunny!" I grumbled. Alice and Junchao shot me a warning with their eyes—I was being negative. "Great idea," I quickly added, trying to save myself.

"Also," Sunny said, "I read that ghosts like it if you look like them a little bit. So I thought we could use Mommy's baby powder to make ourselves look more like the ghost."

"That is a good idea," said Alice. "My grandmother says that ghosts are really vain."

"What does vain mean?" I asked.

"It means conceited or stuck-up," Sunny said.

"A stuck-up ghost?" I said. "You would think that you'd get over yourself by the time you're dead. But I say let's do it."

I took the flashlight from Sunny and found my mom's baby powder in the bathroom cabinet and then dumped some over my head and all over my pajamas. Alice, Junchao, and Sunny did the same. We stood in the bathroom in a giant cloud of powder, coughing. Each of us was wearing our hanger hat filled with pencils and we were now covered in baby powder. Everything about us was white: our pajamas, our arms, our feet, our hair . . . The only thing not white, weirdly, were our eyes.

"Now what?" I asked.

"It says," Sunny read, "'that if your ghost persists to stick around that it may have a reason to stay. The ghost might be trying to communicate with you.'"

"You mean, tell us something?" I asked. "But we already communicated when I tried to ask her, I mean it, to leave."

"That was us telling it something. Not the ghost telling us something," Alice pointed out.

"Exactly," said Sunny. "But it warns that 'you should never try to communicate with the ghost. It says that an inexperienced person might make an error that could open up a portal and cause the ghost to haunt the house forever.'"

"Forever," Junchao moaned, covering her white face with her white hands.

"That's a really long time," Alice said, looking over at me.

"It can't live here forever because we already live here, and . . . truthfully . . . I kind of like it here."

Sunny's eyes opened in surprise. I'd never said this before. Or at least not when my mom didn't ask me.

Sunny and I always told our mom that we liked it here, but we only told her that because we knew she needed us to be okay with the divorce and the move and my dad having a girlfriend and all, and so we said we were. When really, both Sunny and I were secretly hoping that my mom would tell us that this whole divorce thing was off and that we were moving home—to be with my dad and to live in our actual home.

But was I hoping that anymore? I kind of thought that I might not be. I looked around the bathroom. This place was home.

"I like it here too," Sunny said. "Did you know that New Jersey is the largest chemical-producing state in the whole country? And I love chemicals." She smiled at me, and I knew that she wasn't really talking about chemicals.

"I like it here too, since I was born here and it's the only place I've ever lived," said Junchao.

"I like it here too, because you guys are here," Alice said.

"That's the best reason to like it," I told her. *"Gui mi* group hug!"

We all hugged—including Sunny. Our hanger hats clanked together and when we separated, I think Alice's hat had a few of my pencils stuck to it.

Ridding Your House of Unwanted Spirits: Show It the Way

"Okay, let's get to work," I said.

The four of us sat down on the pink bathroom rug. Sunny read from my mom's iPad: "'The first thing you have to do is to cover up all the mirrors in the house with towels and open up all the windows at least an inch.'"

"Cover the mirrors and open the windows?" Junchao asked.

"It says that when you perform the ghost-removal ceremony, you don't want the ghost going into the mirror by accident because then it will be stuck in your house. You want it to go out the window. That's why you open every one of them, to make it easy for the ghost to leave."

"That makes sense," said Alice.

I stood up and opened up the bathroom closet and took out all of our bath towels. "Let's go room by room."

"Can I just stay in this room?" asked Junchao.

"But you'll be alone," I said. "Because we're leaving it."

"Never mind," she said, getting up.

Alice moved over to the bathroom window. She opened it up about two inches. I climbed up on the sink and threw a bath towel over the bathroom mirror. "One room done!" I announced. We all smiled at each other.

Sunny pulled something from her backpack.

"What is that?" I asked.

"It's an electromagnetic field meter," she said. "It measures electromagnetic fields, which are physical fields produced by electrically charged objects."

"Do ghosts not like electricity?" I asked hopefully.

"No, they use electricity," she said. "It should begin to beep if the ghost comes near us."

The thought of that little machine beeping made all the hairs on my arms stand straight up. I picked up my mom's baby powder and gave myself another dose of it. Alice and Junchao did the same.

"Hey," I said. "Why didn't you pull that thing out in the bedroom?"

"It said the first step was to use the bathroom. And I wanted to follow the steps," she said.

I couldn't stop myself. I picked up the baby powder and dumped the whole thing on Sunny.

Junchao gasped.

Alice grabbed the powder from my hands.

Sunny sneezed, causing a pencil to fall from her hat and hit the tile floor with a *plunk*.

"Quick," Junchao said. "Say you're sorry."

Sunny's eyes looked unbelievably spooky shining happily out from her powdery-white face.

"But . . ."

"Hurry, say it," Alice said.

Sunny's white lips turned up in a grin.

I thought my head would explode. But I thought about Trudy and her monster anger, and I managed to get out a tiny "I'm sorry."

Alice and Junchao looked around the bathroom, hoping that this little apology would keep the ghost away.

"I'm sure that Masha was just making me extra safe with the powder," Sunny said. She patted my arm just to rub in the fact that I had to apologize to her. She knew that the touch of her tiny evil hand would totally get to me.

I counted to twenty in Chinese . . . By the time I got to *shi liu*, or sixteen, the danger of walloping little Dr. Freakenstein had faded.

"Let's start with the mirrors and windows at the back of the house and work our way to the living room," Sunny suggested.

"Do we have to do your mother's room?" asked Alice. "Mrs. Song is in there." She looked worried.

"We won't wake her up, Alice," I said. "We will be as quiet as four little mice."

She didn't look convinced, but we couldn't leave the big mirror on my mother's dresser uncovered. And my mom had two giant windows in her room too.

We lined up in front of the bathroom door. I held the flashlight, and Junchao and Sunny held the towels. Once we were all set, I slowly opened the door.

I checked the hall.

Nothing.

I looked back at Sunny's little meter thingy.

It was quiet.

"What happens if that thing goes off?" I whispered. "Maybe you should stay here in the bathroom."

"NO!" she cried. "I'm too scared." She looked up at me with those giant blue eyes of hers and I couldn't make her stay.

"Okay, then stand right outside the door to Mommy's room. Don't come in. Just in case. We don't want to wake up Mrs. Song."

"Yes," Alice said. "We don't want to wake up Mrs. Song," she repeated.

I crept out into the hall. Alice, Sunny, and Junchao followed. We started down the hall toward my mother's room, sticking to the side of the hallway so the floor wouldn't squeak. I'd learned from sneaking out of my bedroom at night for illegal snacks that the middle of the hallway was the squeakiest part. But it was hard to stick close to the wall with our hanger hats on. My pencils kept scraping the wall. If the ghost didn't get us, my mom sure would in the morning for all the pencil marks.

When I got to the door, I took a couple of deep breaths to make up for all the breathing that I wasn't going to do once I got into the bedroom with Mrs. Song. Then I turned the doorknob and slowly opened the door.

SQUEEEEEEAK.

Alice poked me.

I shrugged at her.

"Open it fast," she whispered. "It squeaks less."

I opened it fast. No squeak. I smiled at her. This was good to know.

I peeked over at my mom's bed.

There was Mrs. Song, a sleeping lump on the right-hand side of the bed. I could hear her quiet breathing, in and out, in and out, with a little whistle to the out part. I turned and gave the "shh" sign to Alice, Junchao, and Sunny.

I motioned to Alice, and mimed like I was opening a window.

She got it.

I motioned to Junchao, pointed at the towels she was carrying, and then motioned for her to follow me.

She didn't get it. She blinked in confusion.

I opened my eyes wide and went through the plan again: pointing at the towels, pointing at her, pointing at me, and then pretended to hang an invisible towel over a mirror.

She nodded her head. She got it.

I breathed in deep through my nose to keep myself calm. Then I motioned for Sunny to stay just outside the door with her little machine.

We went to work.

Alice had to open two windows, one on either side of my mother's bed. They were the kind with the crank handles that you had to turn. We had the big mirror over my mom's dresser to cover, plus her little makeup mirror.

Junchao and I crept over to the dresser. I pulled a T-shirt from my mom's dirty clothes and hung it over her makeup mirror. Junchao smiled at me in the dark. The big mirror was going to be a lot harder.

I saw that I was going to have to climb on top of the dresser to get the towel up on each side of the big mirror. I put my hand up to Junchao, telling her to stay. And then I hoisted myself up on the side of the dresser, placing my knee on the corner, and then pulling up my other knee. I still couldn't reach the top of the mirror, so I slowly stood. Junchao handed me one end of the bath towel and I hooked it over the corner of the mirror.

I looked down at Junchao to give her a thumbs-up just as Mrs. Song sniffed and rolled over in bed.

I froze.

If she opened her eyes, she would see me standing on my mother's dresser covered in baby powder and wearing a hanger on my head with pencils sticking out of it.

That might totally freak her out.

She did not open her eyes.

Junchao and I made a "that was too close" face at each other.

Alice was already back at the door with Sunny, done with both her windows. I still needed to get the other corner of the towel over the top of the other side of the mirror. It looked like the best way was for me to stay on the dresser and walk across it to the other side. But the top of my mother's dresser was a mess of perfume and makeup and papers and pens and junk of all kinds. She really needed to clean more. This was going to be hard.

I started across. My first step was perfect, right between some keys and a glass of water.

Out of the corner of my eye, I saw Junchao mouth, "be careful" at me.

My second step wasn't so perfect; I stepped right on top of a lipstick or a mascara or something. It killed my foot to stay on it, but if I didn't, I knew that I'd fall right off the dresser. I quickly took a third step closer to the back of the dresser—

CLANG!

Knocking over a tall bottle of perfume.

Junchao threw herself onto the ground.

Sunny and Alice scooted out the door of the bedroom.

I held my breath . . . hoping that somehow this would make me invisible.

Mrs. Song mumbled. It sounded like it was something about her garden. Then she whispered, "Masha?"

My heart nearly burst. I didn't know what to do. Alice was probably dying behind the door—thinking that it was all over, and she was pretty much on her way home right this minute.

"Masha?" Mrs. Song repeated. This time, I could almost feel her opening her eyes.

"Your hydrangea bushes are beautiful," I whispered. "Especially the blue ones. I love the blue ones."

I heard Mrs. Song sigh. She loved her hydrangea bushes. I think the white ones were her favorites, but mine were the ones with the giant light-blue flowers.

108

They were the color of a Cinderella princess dress. I thought it would be better to stick to the truth in the middle of the night.

It worked.

"Hydrangeas," she whispered. And then she rolled over.

I couldn't help smiling. Mrs. Song sure loved her flowers; she even dreamed about them the way I dreamed about horses.

I looked down at Junchao.

She was staring up at me.

I gave her a nod and then took another step toward the end of the dresser. And then another.

I decided that this was close enough.

Junchao crawled over to the end of the dresser behind me, grabbed the other end of the towel, and then handed it to me behind my back.

I pulled it around me on the side of the mirror, careful not to knock anything else over on my mother's very messy dresser, and then linked it over the top corner of the mirror.

Done.

Now I had to get the heck down from here.

I crouched, found two empty places to put my hands down on the dresser top, and then I sprung off of it, falling onto the carpet into a roll, kicking Junchao accidentally in the stomach and losing my hanger hat. Junchao found it for me. I smashed it back onto my head, scared to be without it. And then the two of us scrambled for the door, squishing out of it together.

Once I got out, Alice whispered in my ear, "I knew you could do it."

I hadn't been so sure.

Junchao closed the door so quietly that the only sound was the tiny snap as the tongue of the door slipped into place. And then all four of us collapsed into a heap on the floor outside my mom's room. We had a bunch more windows and doors to do, but the worst was over.

Then Sunny's machine gave a tiny squawk.

And then another.

And another.

Positively Sparkly

Stop that thing!" Junchao cried.

"I can't," Sunny whispered.

The beeping got louder.

I couldn't decide which to worry about more, that the sound would wake up Mrs. Song or that the ghost was getting closer and closer to us.

Clomp. Clomp. Clomp.

The footsteps of the ghost seemed farther away than they had been before, but still Sunny's machine kept beeping.

I closed my eyes tightly, hoping that if I couldn't see it then it couldn't hurt me.

"Masha!" Junchao yelled. "Do something!"

The beeping grew and grew.

I had no idea what to do. How do you fight off a ghost? Does a ghost punch you? Or does something bad happen, like furniture swirling around or forks and knives from the kitchen chasing you?

The beeping grew even louder.

The sound pressed on me from all sides.

Wooo. Wooo. Wooooo.

Sunny yelped.

I leaped to my feet. This ghost better not touch my little sister.

The beeping stopped.

I searched the dark hallway. I saw nothing. I heard nothing. I breathed, and my heart thumped a bit slower.

"What did you do?" asked Alice.

"I don't know," I said.

"It's gone now," Sunny said.

Junchao yawned.

"How can you be sleepy when we almost came face-to-face with a real ghost?" Alice asked.

Junchao shrugged. And then her belly grumbled. "I'm hungry too." She laughed. "Ho- ho-ho." I loved her laugh.

"Shh," Alice hissed at her. But I could see her covering a smile with her hand.

"Let's get back to work," I said, trying to keep us focused. "We need that ghost out of here."

I picked up the bath towels that were all over the floor and walked into my room. I flicked on the light switch out of habit. But of course, the light did not come on. My closet door was closed, thank goodness. I checked out the rest of the dark corners of my room. Nothing strange or scary. So I walked to my window over my desk, moved my desk chair out a little, and stood on it to open the window. Cool night air hit my face, along with a light misty spray of rain. It felt good.

When I turned around, Junchao and Alice were hanging a towel over the mirror on my dresser. It was a small one compared to my mom's, so it was much easier. Sunny stood by them holding her ghost-meter thingy. She looked over at me and smiled. I smiled back. We had to get rid of this ghost.

Next, we headed into Sunny's room and opened her window. She didn't have a mirror.

All we had left was the kitchen, living room, and dining room. I wasn't looking forward to this part because the ghost had to be in one of them. I guessed it could have been down in the basement by the washing machine and dryer, or in the spidery storage area where my mom kept boxes and boxes of stuff that we never used. That would actually be the perfect place for a ghost. But something kept telling me that she was in that front hall closet.

"We should head to the kitchen," I whispered, hoping someone had a better idea.

Sunny did.

"Wait," she said. "I think Trudy can feel us working to get rid of her."

"Stop calling her that," I whined.

Alice and Junchao eyeballed me.

114

"It might be a good idea to protect ourselves more with stuff like the hangers and the powder," said Sunny.

"That is a good idea," Junchao said.

"Like what?" I asked.

"I know," said Alice. "My grandmother said that when she was a kid, they used to fill their pockets with raw meat. It protects you from bad spirits, and also demons."

"What about wild dogs?" I asked.

"I don't know about that," Alice said.

I loved my friends, but neither of them could take a joke.

"I'm a vegetarian," Sunny said, not looking up from the iPad.

"You don't have to eat it. You just have to wear it," Alice pointed out.

"I'm not wearing bloody meat," Junchao said.

"Me neither," I said.

"Listen," said Sunny. "This site says that ghosts don't like shiny objects." She looked up and shrugged.

"Let's put necklaces and stuff on," said Junchao.

"I have all my grandmother's fake jewelry in my room," I said. "Follow me."

I mean, I liked anything that protected us more, but necklaces sounded so much better than a pocketful of meat. And I liked not going into the kitchen or living room just yet. I wasn't ready to face the ghost again, especially now that we might know who she was.

The four of us filed into my room. The jewelry was in a box in my closet. Shoot. I didn't like the idea of opening up my closet door.

"Shine the flashlight on my door," I told Sunny.

I walked over and put my hand on the door handle. I breathed a couple of times but still couldn't bring myself to open it.

I heard metal scraping the floor behind me. It was Alice.

"I'm here," she said, standing next to me.

Alice was so much braver than I was. She knew she couldn't run if anything bad came out of that door. I turned to smile at her. She looked a little creepy in the

116

light of the flashlight—shadows ran across her face, making her eyes dark and scary.

"What?" she asked.

"Nothing," I said, turning back to the door.

I swung open the door in one big pull . . . squinting . . . waiting for something to jump out at us.

Nothing did.

"Give me the flashlight, Sunny."

I shined it into my closet. Everything looked normal.

"Can you hold it for me?" I handed it to Alice.

And then I threw a few of my sweaters off the shelf to uncover the box of jewelry that my grandmother gave me. We took the box to the desk and opened it.

"Wow!" Junchao said when she saw all the jewelry inside. It was like a treasure chest. It had necklaces and rings and bracelets and the kind of earrings that snapped onto your ears. All of it was big, because that is the kind of stuff my babushka liked to wear. But more important, all of it was very, very shiny . . . and it wasn't raw meat.

We dug in. I put on about ten necklaces and two rings. The bracelets were a little too much, so I left those off. For my ears, I chose big diamond clip-ons. They pinched a tiny bit, but if they protected me, I was good with the pain.

Alice put on a giant silver locket and red sparkly clip-on earrings and a few bracelets that jingled when she moved.

Junchao went nuts. She covered herself in necklaces and bracelets and rings and earrings. She was like a bejeweled Christmas tree. She even hung some bracelets from her hanger hat!

Sunny put on a necklace and a couple of rings.

We were all pretty shiny.

I caught Sunny's eye. "Thanks," I mouthed. I knew how much Sunny disliked stuff that wasn't science, and this was definitely stuff that wasn't science. She was being so helpful. My little sister was okay.

All of a sudden it hit me . . . I was having positive thoughts about Sunny! This ghost didn't stand a chance.

"Let's finish this job," I said.

A Ghost-Hunting
Knot

All of us lined up at my door. I had the flashlight. Sunny had her backpack of stuff. Alice had her crutches. And Junchao had Alice.

We were each wearing our hanger hats, we were covered in jewelry, and we were glowing white from the baby powder. Our little line crept together down the hall and into the kitchen, our jewelry clinking the whole way.

Once in the kitchen, I remembered that thought I had about the forks and knives coming after me, and I didn't like being in the kitchen at all. I quickly put down the flashlight and jumped up on the sink and opened the window. The kitchen had no mirrors. I jumped down, my necklaces jingling, picked up the flashlight, and whispered for everyone to get ready to move again.

All we had left were the living room and dining room. There were two windows in each and one mirror. But the mirror was on top of the piano right by the front hall closet. Just thinking about it put a cramp in my heart.

I turned around before we walked out of the kitchen and whispered to my bejeweled team. "Let's open the dining room windows first, and then the windows in the living room. We'll cover the mirror over the piano last. And then let's head back into the bathroom to re-powder ourselves. Got it?"

Their nodding faces glowed in the beam of the flashlight. I turned around and headed out into the living room.

Four windows, one mirror. We could do this.

We entered the living room. I stopped for one second by the armchair and everyone bumped into me.

120

"Sorry," I whispered.

I started around the chair and over into the dining room, keeping my feet as far away from the chair skirt, and the little men, as I could.

There weren't too many dark hiding places in the dining room because there was only the dresser thing that held my mom's nice dishes, along with the table and chairs. We walked around the table on the side without the dresser thing. I wasn't taking any chances—a ghost could hide anywhere. The windows were big. I took one and Alice took the other.

We were getting so close! Two more windows and one mirror to go.

Getting back into formation, we headed over to the living room windows. I remembered Sunny hiding behind the drapes. That seemed like days ago. How I wish we could go back to when we thought Sunny howling behind some drapes was about as close to a real ghost as we'd ever get.

Again, Alice took one window and I took the other. Again, we reformed our line.

One mirror to go.

I shined the flashlight on the mirror over the piano.

Then I shined my flashlight on the front hall closet. The door seemed like it had opened up even more since earlier.

I shined the flashlight back on the mirror over the piano.

"What are you doing?" Alice asked.

"Stalling," I told her.

"Did you see anything . . . by the closet?" she asked.

"No," I told her. And I heard Junchao sigh.

"Let's cover the side away from the closet first," I said. "Then we'll do that other side."

I still couldn't make myself move.

"You're doing great, Masha," Sunny said.

I smiled down at my little sister.

"That's good," whispered Junchao. "The ghost won't like all this positive energy."

"Group hug," Alice said.

We all came together in a big clinking-and-clanging hug. But when we pulled away, we were a tangled mess of jewelry.

"Oh no," I whispered.

"Shine the flashlight," Junchao said. Her little fingers tried to untangle us. "I can't do it."

I didn't like standing here like this. We were like a tasty ghost snack just waiting to be eaten. I couldn't stop myself from picturing Trudy Day floating at us with her mouth open and her sharp teeth gleaming in the moonlight, and I lost it . . . I grabbed the three of them and dragged them toward the piano mirror.

"Ouch," Alice cried.

"My hair," Junchao yelled.

"Towel," I whispered.

Junchao handed me one.

I only had one hand because I was using the other to hold on to everyone, so I shook the towel open and tossed it up and over the mirror.

"Oh no," Alice said.

"What?" I asked. I couldn't turn to see.

"It slipped behind the piano," Sunny whispered.

"Towel," I shouted to Junchao.

"It's the last one," she said.

I ripped it from her hands and shook it out. My neck ached from our human knot, my heart beat as if it had a monster truck motor in it, and I was sweating like a marathon runner. *I can do this. I can do this. I can do this.*

CLOMP. CLOMP. CLOMP.

This time the footsteps of the ghost sounded as if they were right on top of us. I threw the towel up into the air without aiming.

"You did it!" Alice cried.

Wooo. Wooo. Wooooo.

We didn't hang around to celebrate.

I dragged our clump the heck away from the front hall closet and back down the hall—tripping and stepping on each other the entire way to the bathroom.

Once inside, we fell onto the bathroom rug in a panting hot mess of jewelry, hangers, pencils, and powder. I closed the door as quietly as I could with my foot.

We certainly didn't look like professional ghost hunters. But we had done it!

When Flushing Doesn't Work

I shined the flashlight while Alice worked to separate us.

"Can't we just snap the chains?" asked Sunny, while she bent over my mom's iPad, reading.

"No," I said. "This is Babushka's stuff." Although if Alice couldn't get us untangled soon, I was thinking that we might have to break some of it.

Junchao leaned her head against the bathroom wall. Her eyes were closed. "You tired, Junchao?" I asked. "Junchao? Junchao!"

She snorted awake. "What? The ghost? Where?"

"Junchao!" I yelled. "How could you fall asleep?"

"She is experiencing sleep deprivation and so is *microsleeping*. That is, taking short little periods of sleep to make up for not getting enough sleep," Sunny said.

"That's right," Junchao said. "I'm microsleeping because it's after three in the morning." She yawned. "Isn't the ghost going to leave now anyway?"

"They don't just leave on their own," Sunny said. "We just made it possible for Trudy to leave by opening the windows and covering the mirrors. Now we have to get her to leave."

I groaned. "Stop calling it that."

I was actually in need of a little microsleep myself.

"So . . . how do we do that, Sunny? Do I have to ask it again?"

"Well, there seems to be a list of ways to do it. You can wish the ghost gone on an old spoon. You can clap your hands three times in every room in the house."

"I've heard of that one," Alice said. "My grandmother is always clapping her hands."

126

"It says that you can even vacuum the house," added Sunny.

I turned to Alice. "So ghosts don't like vacuum cleaners?"

Alice shrugged. "How should I know?"

"I just thought since your grandmother . . . never mind," I said.

"There are more," Sunny continued. "You can flush your toilet ten times."

"Let's try that one," said Junchao.

Sunny kept reading. "Or you can sprinkle a mixture of dill and salt and fennel in front of all your doors to draw the ghost out."

"What's fennel?" I asked.

"It even says that if everyone in the house chews on cloves and then spits out the window, then the ghost will go."

"I don't know if we can convince Mrs. Song to spit out the window in the middle of the night," I said.

"But the most effective way to get a ghost to leave," read Sunny, "is to travel out into the night in sight of the moon and gather tall grass. And then go

127

to where you believe the ghost resides and tie a knot in the grass. And then you are to take that grass and bury it in the dirt to confine the spirit to its grave."

"Let's just flush the toilet," I said.

Junchao hopped up. She leaned over and flushed the toilet once. And then again. And again. And then four more times. She tried it for the eighth time, but nothing happened. "Try jiggling the handle," Alice suggested.

Junchao jiggled it.

Then she tried to flush it.

Nothing.

She jiggled it again.

And then tried to flush it again.

Nothing.

I threw my face into my hands and moaned. Of course it couldn't be as easy as flushing a toilet.

"Let's try the spoon thing," Junchao said.

"We need to go outside. Sunny said it's the best way to get rid of it." I adjusted my jewelry and my hanger hat and pencils. Then I stood up and got the powder back out and gave myself another dose.

Alice got up and did the same.

"Wait! No!" Junchao wailed. "Let's spit. Let's spit."

When we didn't answer her, she sighed and took the powder from Alice and poured it over her long black hair. Sunny stuck her monitor in her pocket and powdered up as well.

I looked out the bathroom window into the dark. It had stopped raining, but there was still the popping sound of the raindrops falling from the trees.

"I say that we head into Mrs. Song's yard. She has that long grass in her back garden over by her pond. Do you know it, Sunny?"

"You mean the *Pennisetum ruppelii*," Sunny said. "Or, as it's more commonly known, fountain grass."

"Or even more commonly known as *long grass*," I said, frowning.

"Masha!" Junchao said.

"Oh yeah, I forgot." I sighed. I was getting really tired. And because I still sounded a little negative, I added, "Let's go dig us up some fountain grass." Sunny was actually being terrific tonight. I should cut her some slack.

The route we needed to take to the grass was out the back door, because I wanted to avoid the front door and the closet. Going out the back made it harder to get into Mrs. Song's yard because we'd have to walk into the little woods behind our houses so we could get around the fence that separated our yards. But I'd still rather do that than risk running into the ghost that was probably sitting right behind my mom's umbrellas in the front hall closet.

But going through the woods was not so much the real problem, even though it did sound kind of scary in the middle of the night. The real problem was Alice's crutches. How would she get through the woods with those things?

The edge of the woods was thick with bushes, old dried leaves, and fallen branches. Both my mom and Mrs. Song threw all the old leaves and sticks that fell in our yards back there, so it made it hard to walk through. For Alice, it would be nearly impossible.

I looked at the broken toilet. Why couldn't that have worked?

130

I had no idea how to get Alice through the woods, so I figured that I'd get us out there and hope an idea came to me then.

"Line up," I said. "We're going to go out the back door."

"But if we go out the back, then we have to get around the backyard fence by going through the woods," Sunny said.

Why did my sister always have to know everything?

"Through the woods?" Alice said.

"We'll figure it out," I said. "Let's go."

Alice smiled, her mouth made that curvy shape I loved, but I could see the sadness sitting behind it. She was trying to tell me that she had to stay here.

Junchao got it too.

"No," Junchao said. "We can't separate. You know what happens if we do."

She was right. We'd all seen enough movies to know exactly what would happen if we separated. We'd be doomed, goners, the ghost would have us all.

"You three go," Alice said. "I'll stay here in the bathroom."

I stood there, my brain whirling.

"Plus, I can keep trying to flush the toilet."

"No, we all go," I said.

"How, Masha?" Junchao asked.

"What about the wheelbarrow?" Sunny suggested. "Mommy keeps it right outside the back door against the house. We can wheel Alice through the woods."

"Great idea, Sunny!" I patted her on the shoulder. I had to remember this moment. Sunny Sweet could so get on my nerves, but tonight she was really saving us.

"The wheelbarrow?" Alice said. But I was already lining us up at the door.

I cracked the door open about two inches and pointed the flashlight out into the hallway. And then I turned around and nodded to my posse. We started out and down the hallway again and back into the kitchen. I took us straight to the back door.

"Should we try the wishing on the spoon thing, since we're here?" Junchao asked.

I looked out the kitchen window into our dark backyard. I didn't like the thought of all the forks and knives chasing us around the house, but the idea of *traveling out into the night in sight of the moon* was freaking me out even more right now. I opened up the utensil drawer.

First, I picked up a tablespoon. But then I put it back and picked up my mom's giant spoon that she serves ice cream with. This was better. I turned around and handed Sunny the flashlight. "What do I do?"

"It just says to wish the ghost gone," she said.

I shrugged. And then I held the big spoon in both my hands and closed my eyes, which felt like the right position for a wish.

"Be polite," Alice whispered. "My grandmother says that sometimes ghosts have been haunting around so long that they've forgotten they're dead. So maybe you should remind her nicely, and that this is your home now, and it's time to move on to the light."

I opened up one eye. "What's the light?"

Alice took her hand from her crutch and pointed up.

I closed my eye and took a big breath and said, "Dear ghost—"

"You should call her Trudy," Sunny whispered.

"I don't want to," I whispered back. And then I started again. "Dear ghost, I hope you're having a good night."

Junchao gave a snort.

"We are not having the best night because . . ." Now how to say this nicely? "We're not sure if you remember this or not, but you're . . ." I didn't want to use the word *dead*. It seemed kind of harsh. "You've passed away." I hugged the big ice cream spoon to my chest. "And it's time that you moved on . . . to the light." I gestured up to the sky with the spoon, just in case the ghost didn't know which direction the light was. "I bet it's a really nice place up there. I bet it's like Disneyland, only with free soda and no lines at the Twilight Zone Tower of Terror ride."

Alice cleared her throat. Maybe I was getting off track a bit.

"So, again, about the light. We were thinking . . . actually, we were wishing that you would take that nice trip up into the air toward the light." I squeezed the spoon tightly in my hands. "And we wish that you would do it, um, now."

I was afraid to open my eyes. After a few seconds of silence, I blinked them open. Sunny, Junchao, Alice, and I were standing in the middle of the kitchen in a tight little circle. Sunny was the last one to open her eyes. Then all four of us stood blinking in the light of the flashlight. The kitchen clock ticked away on the wall. None of us moved.

Was it over? Maybe it was over. It could be over. And we didn't have to go outside into the light of the moon!

But then it happened.

CLOMP. CLOMP. CLOMP.

It's like the ghost was walking around in the same place and for the same amount of time, almost as if it were doing some weird dance move.

Wooo. Wooo. Wooooo.

I quickly slammed the utensil drawer shut before the forks and knives could get out.

The Wheelbarrow Probably Wasn't a Good Idea

The kitchen door opened up with a loud squeak. The sound would have made my heart start pounding, but the thought of going out into the dark night already had it beating away. Even the wet night air smelled spooky.

All four of us piled onto our tiny wooden back porch. It took me and Junchao holding onto each of Alice's elbows to help her down the step from the kitchen door to the porch. There was a little roof over the porch so it was dry. Sunny held the flashlight and a bunch of kitchen towels I told her to grab in case the wheelbarrow was wet. I closed the door behind us.

Sunny shined the flashlight out into the yard. The beam of light only made it about halfway across, making the yard seem so much bigger than I remembered it being yesterday. Our swing set, which was blue and pink and happy in the sunshine of the day, looked like a giant metal monster crouching in the corner of the yard under the big tree. The big tree, which I loved to climb just about every day of my life, seemed as if it were bending and stretching its branches, getting ready to grab us. I was glad that we didn't have to go anywhere near them. I looked over to where we did have to go, toward the shed.

For the first time ever, I noticed exactly how scary our shed looked. It was short, fat, and wooden, with a door that didn't close right because it wasn't the right fit for the shed. Sunny had destroyed the real door this past spring. She said that she was doing experiments on turning wood into gas. I don't know if the shed door turned into gas, but it did turn into a black and twisted mess. Mom left it out for the trash men and put an old closet door that we had down in the basement on the shed.

But because it wasn't the right kind, it didn't go all the way down to the bottom of the frame, so there was a three- or four-inch gap at the bottom. When I stared at it in the dark, I swear that I saw the shadow of feet under the door. And we had to pass right by that shed to go into the woods to get around the fence and into Mrs. Song's yard.

I looked for our wheelbarrow. The moon lit up the back side of our house, making the windows look like dark eyes staring out into the yard. The wheelbarrow leaned against the side of the house between the windows, making it look like a giant nose.

"Wait here," I said. I stepped off the porch and walked along the wet pavement toward the wheelbarrow; my jewelry clanked in the night like the bones of a skeleton. I held the chains to stop them from making the scary bone sound.

The wheelbarrow was under the eaves of the house, and it didn't look too wet. I reached for the handles . . .

138

but then I remembered the millions of daddy longlegs that liked to hang out against the back of the house, and I turned and ran back to the porch.

"What's wrong?" Alice asked.

"I need the flashlight."

I wasn't going to mention the daddy longlegs to poor Alice. I might have to touch the wheelbarrow, but she had to sit in it.

Sunny handed me the flashlight, and I ran back to the wheelbarrow and shined it all around. I didn't see any spiders. I put the flashlight down in the grass so its beam shot up into the sky, and then I grabbed the handles of the wheelbarrow and pulled it from the house. Something ran up my bare arm.

I dropped the wheelbarrow and jumped back from the house, tripping over the flashlight and falling right on my butt in the cold, wet grass. The wheelbarrow clanged against the house while it fell. It was loud enough to wake the dead, but then I remembered the dead were already awake. But it was also loud enough to wake Mrs. Song as a metal ring echoed through the silent neighborhood.

Sunny, Junchao, and Alice all crouched together in a heap on the porch with their hands covering their ears.

We waited.

A dog barked from down the street. Then a far-off beep of a car horn. And then nothing but the breeze blowing through the tops of the trees in the little woods in the back of our yard and the sound of plopping raindrops hitting the leaves on the ground.

"The ghost is going to die of old age before we get it out of here," complained Junchao.

"How can something die if it's already dead?" I grumbled.

I picked up my hanger hat and put it on, and then I wiped at my arms and legs to be sure there was nothing crawling on me. My pajama bottoms sagged a bit in the butt from getting wet when I fell. Then I set the wheelbarrow straight, put the flashlight in it, and wheeled it over to the porch. "Your chariot, my princess."

Alice stood up but didn't let go of her crutches.

"I think you should leave your crutches here," Junchao said.

140

Alice didn't look like she was into this idea.

"We'll be with you the whole time," I told her.

She leaned her crutches against the door and gave me a smile. And this time, the curling shape of her lips didn't hide any sadness; it was all happy.

Sunny jumped down from the porch and plucked the flashlight from the wheelbarrow and then put all the kitchen towels down in the bottom of it. Then Junchao and I first helped Alice into a sitting position onto the porch, and then up and into the wheelbarrow.

"Sunny," I said, "give Alice the flashlight. And you and Junchao get on either side of the wheelbarrow so I don't tip it. I'll push."

Sunny handed Alice the flashlight. The two of them took their positions on either side of the wheelbarrow. "Ready?" I asked.

Alice turned around and looked at me. "I'm pretty sure that this is one of the things that my mom and dad were afraid of when they said they didn't want me sleeping over." She laughed.

Junchao joined in with her loud, "Ho-ho-ho." Even Sunny couldn't keep herself from laughing.

141

We did look pretty funny . . . the four of us in our pajamas, wearing hangers and pencils on our heads and covered in baby powder and sparkly jewels, with Alice riding in a wheelbarrow out into the wet woods in the middle of the night.

We started out. I pushed the wheelbarrow toward the shed, hoping that the hangers and the pencils and the powder and the jewelry worked on shed monsters as well as ghosts.

When we got close to it, I picked up speed. Alice clung to the sides of the wheelbarrow. Because I was pretty scared, I was having trouble keeping the wheelbarrow steady. We hit a big stick, and the wheelbarrow leaned toward Junchao. Junchao caught the side of it in her hands and kept it from tipping over.

"Be careful, Masha!" she said in a whisper.

But we were past the monster in the shed. My heart stopped pounding, and I calmed down enough to grab the handles of the wheelbarrow tighter. We were almost at the edge of the woods.

I pushed Alice toward the line of forsythia bushes. "Close your eyes, everyone," I said. I closed mine too, which maybe was not the best idea.

We went under.

All the long branches scraped across my face and body, catching on my necklaces and just about knocking off my hanger hat. One long branch wrapped around my ankle as I shoved at the wheelbarrow. It wouldn't let me go, and I tripped out of the bushes on the other side, landing on the cool dirt that surrounded the bushes. The wheelbarrow slid to its side, dumping Alice on top of Sunny.

"I'm so sorry. I'm so sorry," I howled.

Junchao scrambled to help Alice and Sunny. I got up and righted the wheelbarrow. And then picked up the flashlight. We were all okay, at least mostly anyway. Although we had lost a few pencils from our hanger hats and gained a few wet leaves.

Alice looked pretty shaken up. Junchao squeaked that she wanted to go home. And Sunny stared at me, waiting for me to say something. I knew what I had to say. I just didn't want to say it. But I did.

"You guys," I started. But they didn't stop grumbling. "YOU GUYS!" I said louder. They stopped and looked up at me. "We need to head back to the house. You three are going to sit on the porch, and I'm going to run over to Mrs. Song's to get the grass by myself."

Junchao gasped.

"No!" Alice said.

Sunny didn't say anything.

"We have to do it this way. I'm not strong enough to push the wheelbarrow over the leaves and sticks in the woods. I'm so sorry, Alice." I felt like such a failure. "And I don't like the idea of leaving the three of you out here without Alice's crutches. We need to go back."

It was quiet as we each thought about things in the dark. We all knew that I was right.

I turned the wheelbarrow around, and Junchao and I helped Alice back into it. She shined the flashlight ahead of us, and this time I kept control of myself. I wasn't going to dump Alice back onto the wet ground, even if a zombie came out of that shed and started chomping on my leg. We slowly made our way back through the forsythia bushes and past the shed. A zombie did not come out. Although I'm almost sure I heard one moaning in there.

In about five minutes, we were back to the house. Sunny held onto the wheelbarrow, and Junchao and I helped Alice out and then up the two stairs of the porch. I could almost hear Alice's parents sigh in their sleep all the way across town. Junchao climbed onto the porch and took a seat next to Alice. Sunny stood by the wheelbarrow.

I blinked at my friends and my little sister in the dark.

After all the hours we'd battled this ghost together . . . this was good-bye.

Being a Hero Is Lonely

I'll be fine," I told them. Even though I was pretty sure that within a few minutes, I'd be a late-night snack for the monster in the shed. No one mentioned how we were not supposed to separate, or any of the bad things that happened when you did. Maybe this was why it always happened in the movies . . . because there was some big reason why they couldn't stay together.

Maybe.

Or maybe not.

But for us, I didn't see any other way.

I took the flashlight from Sunny. "See ya," I said. But the "ya" got stuck in my throat so it sounded like I just said "see."

Alice grabbed me in a big hug. Junchao joined in. And then Sunny did too. I was being smothered by love and poked by a few pencils at the same time. It felt good. Even the pencil pokes. Their hugs made me feel strong. I could do this.

I turned and walked off as soon as they let me go so they didn't see the tears in my eyes. Heroes didn't cry, did they?

It was amazing how fast I got past the scary shed without a big wheelbarrow to push. Then I held my hanger hat on with one hand and ducked under the forsythia bushes. I stood at the edge of the woods and shined the flashlight through the trees.

"You have to go in there," I whispered to myself.

But I didn't. I didn't have to go. Just like Junchao, I wanted to go home. I turned around and started back into the forsythia.

I couldn't do this. I didn't want to do this. The branches scraped at my face. I got down on my hands

147

and knees and crawled in the dirt. The light of the flashlight bobbed about wildly next to me, making the world unsteady. I lost track of what was up and what was down. I rolled out of the bushes and into something small and soft. Sunny Sweet.

"What are you doing?" she asked.

"What are *you* doing?" I asked back.

"Coming with you," she said.

"No," I said. But I didn't mean it. I wanted her to come. I didn't want to be alone.

She smiled down at me. I got up off the ground. Even before I was done standing up and wiping the dirt off my pajamas and pushing my stupid hanger hat back on my head for the millionth time tonight, I knew that I needed to take Sunny back to the house.

"Sunny," I said.

She cut me off. "I know, Masha. You're sending me back to Alice and Junchao." She sighed as she leaned down and picked up my flashlight and handed it to me. And then she handed me something else. It was small and soft.

"What's this?" I asked.

"It's a rabbit's foot," she said.

"A good-luck charm? Whose is it?" I asked.

"It's mine," she said.

"What?"

"I know." She hung her little head. "It's crazy superstitious to have one. But"—she looked up at me—"it's actually Daddy's. I took it from him when we moved. Don't you remember that he used it as a key chain for his car keys?"

Now I remembered. I nodded my head. Every time my father went to start the car, Sunny would lecture him about the stupid foot and how unscientific superstitions were. It made my heart hurt to think of Sunny taking it with her to New Jersey. The whole divorce had seemed so crazy, and so my little sister had done a crazy thing to make herself feel better.

"Take it. It will keep you safe," she said.

I squeezed the foot in my hand. And then I tied it to my pajamas using the strings from my pants.

"If you go back into the woods a little farther in," Sunny said, "the leaves won't be as deep and it will be easier to walk. That way, you will also meet up with

149

that little path that Mrs. Song made into the woods. It goes straight to her illegal goldfish pond."

Mrs. Song hated rules. Especially when it got in the way of her garden. She had learned that because of some laws, she wasn't allowed to build a pond for her goldfish. But she'd built it anyway; she just built it farther into the woods so it wouldn't get noticed.

"Most of Mrs. Song's *Pennisetum ruppelii* is growing around the pond."

"Okay," I said. "I'll take that way." I smiled at her and turned to go.

"Masha," Sunny said, reaching for my arm.

"Yeah, Sunny?"

"I love you," she said.

"Are you telling me this because you don't think I'm going to make it?" I asked, afraid that she might say yes.

"You are totally going to make it," she said. "Remember, Masha, I know everything."

I gave my little sister a hug and then watched her run back past the shed and over to the two dark figures of Alice and Junchao sitting on the porch.

When she got there, she threw her hand up in a big wave. I waved back. And then I turned around and started under the forsythia bushes for the third time tonight.

Sunny was right. She was always right. I could do this thing. I yawned. That is, if I could stay awake long enough to get the grass and get back to the house.

I did what Sunny said and made my way deeper into the woods to get past all the leaves and sticks at the edge of our yards. I wished I'd brought a jacket because all the branches scraping at my arms made me think of daddy longlegs, which kept freaking me out. The world in front of my cold, wet feet was lit up by the flashlight, but all around me was darkness.

When I got in far enough, I turned to my right and started toward where the little path should be. After a minute or two of walking, I shined the flashlight up ahead of me to see if I could spot the path. Before I could see anything up ahead of me, my toe hit something hard and I fell into a bunch of leaves and old branches. It was like the tenth time I'd been in the wet dirt tonight. But this time, I wasn't alone. Something long and skinny wiggled underneath me.

I leaped up so fast and so high that I hit my hanger hat on a tree branch. Which was good for two reasons. One, because being stunned by pain from a hanger digging into my skull kept me from screaming loud enough to wake up everyone in the entire neighborhood. And two, it gave me something to hang on to so my feet weren't anywhere near the ground and the slithery thing down there in the leaves.

I hung in the tree, breathing . . . and waiting for whatever that thing was to get to its home. I was hoping that it had one and that it was far away from this tree. But then I remembered the flashlight. Where was it? It must have been knocked off when I fell.

I let go of the branch and dropped onto the ground. I didn't move my feet for a minute or two, giving the squirmy thing time to realize that I was back. Then I began searching the dark ground for the flashlight. It couldn't have gone too far. But it was hard to see anything. The moon was up there, but so were the tree branches, blocking it.

I felt around with my hands. I didn't want to, but I didn't see that I had any choice. The damp cold of the leaves made them feel slick and icky. Where was that dumb flashlight? I got down onto my knees so I could swipe my hands in a bigger circle.

It was just gone.

I'd have to go on without it.

I stood up and looked around. Which way was Mrs. Song's? Which way was my house? My heart stopped. Oh no. How had I done this? How could I have gotten myself lost?

I took a bunch of steps forward. But then I stopped. It was so dark up ahead. Maybe this was just going deeper into the woods.

I turned and started the other way.

This way was also dark.

"I'm lost. I'm lost," I repeated, hopping in a circle. It felt like the darkness was getting closer to me and the night air was hot and sticky and wouldn't let me breathe. I blinked and blinked, trying to stop the world from squishing into me. I looked up. And then I jumped up . . . and started to climb.

At first my hands and feet didn't even feel the tree, but as I climbed higher and higher, I started to feel better.

I would be able to see up there. I would be able to find my way.

I couldn't tell exactly how high I was, but the branches were getting thinner and the leaves thicker. I stopped and looked around me.

There it was! My house. And Mrs. Song's.

I couldn't see Alice, Junchao, and Sunny on the porch, but I could see Mrs. Song's goldfish pond. It was in a clearing in the trees about a hundred feet away. I could even see the little path that led out of the woods to it. I held onto my hanger hat and looked up at the sky. It was filled with stars. I bet if Sunny were here, she would be able to tell the right way to go just by looking up at these guys. I wanted to feel angry at her for being able to do this, or maybe at myself for not being able to do it. But all I felt was awe for all of the things that my little sister knew how to do.

I couldn't use the stars, so I used my chin instead. I pointed it in the right direction, and then I started down the tree, keeping my chin pointed in the direction of Mrs. Song's pond.

When I dropped out of the tree, I didn't even care if I stepped right on that slimy thing from before. All I cared about was following my chin.

I took off through the dark woods, heading straight in the direction of my chin. I didn't even want to move to pass by a tree, but I obviously had to. My heart pounded so loudly that it just about drowned out the sound of my clanging chains. I kept walking and clanging, walking and clanging. And then I stepped right out onto the path!

It was the most beautiful sight I'd ever seen in my whole life. I laughed out loud and then got down on my hands and knees and kissed the black mulch, which was pretty stupid because it could totally have given my lip a splinter. And then I hopped up and ran for the pond.

The path was dark, but it was still so much easier than walking through the woods. It had lots of little twists and turns in it. Mrs. Song loved things that twisted and turned. Even the walk up to her front door was twisty. She said that all the curves that a twisty path made were just more places she could plant flowers. I knew that there were a bunch of big clumps of tall grass growing right on the side of the pond. I began skipping when I knew I was close. I turned the corner and there she was. Trudy Day!

Trudy with a Fishing Net?

I crouched down on the path.

Her back was to me.

I could tell that she didn't know I was here.

She was small and glowed a bit in the moonlight. And she was bent over the pond and seemed to be studying something in the water.

Maybe she was going to drown me!

I shook inside my pajamas.

Should I run back?

Should I call out to Junchao and Alice?

I held tightly to all the necklaces so my shaking didn't make any jingling sounds. The jewels jabbed into my palms.

She turned.

My heart skipped about ten beats.

She was holding something. A fork? A knife? A little fishing net?

She held a little fishing net.

And it looked familiar. Not the net, but the ghost. It had skinny little arms and legs and wore pajamas.

It was Sunny Sweet!

"Sunny," I called.

The little glowing spirit looked up at me, and then it waved its net and smiled.

I trotted over. "What are you doing here?"

"You were gone so long," she said. "I told Junchao and Alice that I was going inside to use the bathroom, but I really ran out the front door and over here to look for you."

"How did you get past the ghost in the closet?" I asked.

"I ran. I was really worried about you."

"Thanks, Sunny." I smiled. "But you shouldn't have. I bet Junchao and Alice are going crazy right now." That's when I noticed she was still holding the net. "What are you doing with that net?"

"It's not a net. It's actually part of my protozoan culture kit. I thought that if I had to wait for you for a while, I might get some samples. I've been trying to identify the different protozoans in Mrs. Song's pond for months now."

"What?"

"There are more than fifty thousand different species of protozoa, and I am in the middle of . . ."

"Sunny," I interrupted. "How can you be collecting stuff when there is a ghost running around?"

She blinked at me for a few seconds. Then she said, "Habits are pretty powerful."

I rolled my eyes. But then I remembered not to be negative. "Okay, whatever. Put down the culture thingy and let's get what we came for, the long grass." I walked around the other side of the pond and plucked out a bunch of the long grass. I made sure to pull them from different clumps so I didn't mess up Mrs. Song's garden.

"Let's go," I said. I started for the woods. Sunny may have made it past Trudy in her closet, but I wasn't going to try it.

"Where's the flashlight?" she asked.

"I lost it."

"How are we going to get back?" she asked.

"Some smart person told me to walk back into the woods a bit and meet up with Mrs. Song's path to her pond." I smiled. "I thought that we'd take the same way back, only this time I don't plan on getting lost."

"How?" she asked.

"Because I have a little scientist with me who can probably find her way from here to Africa on foot!" I laughed.

"You can't get to Africa on foot," she said. "But I can use science to get us back to our house."

It was my turn to ask the question. "How?"

"$F = G \times m_1 m_2 / r^2$," she said.

"Never mind, I don't want to know."

"The law of gravity," she said. "Come on."

I followed Sunny down the path toward Mrs. Song's yard. "I don't want to go in the front door, Sunny," I whispered at her back.

"Don't worry," she said over her shoulder.

Whenever Sunny told me not to worry, it made me worry more. But I didn't have any other ideas, so I kept following her.

We came out of the woods and into Mrs. Song's yard by the tree that had giant heart-shaped leaves and that got little white flowers on it at the end of every school year. Sunny headed straight for the wooden fence between our yard and Mrs. Song's. Then she walked along it until she came to a group of bushes.

"Now what?" I asked, not really wanting to know.

"Inside the bushes is Mrs. Song's condenser fan for her air conditioner."

I blinked at Sunny in the dark, refusing to say "What?"

161

"I thought we could use the force of gravity to get back into our yard," she continued.

I put my hands on my hips and tapped my foot.

"We climb up onto the condenser and jump over the fence," she said.

I stopped toe tapping and thought about it. Where we were standing in Mrs. Song's part of the yard was almost even with our porch in our yard. In other words, we wouldn't even have to walk past the scary monster in the shed!

"Not a bad idea," I told Sunny.

She smiled so big, the moonlight made her teeth glow.

I pushed my way through the thick, wet, pine-needly bushes with Sunny behind me. In the middle of the bushes was a big machine sitting on a thick square of cement. I climbed up on the cement and then put my toes inside the grates on the side of the machine and climbed up on top of it. I could easily see over the fence and into our yard. What I couldn't see was Alice and Junchao sitting on our porch. But maybe it was just too dark.

I reached down and grabbed Sunny's cold little hand and dragged her up the side of the machine so she was standing on top of it next to me.

"I'll jump over first," I told her. "You stand here and hold on."

I easily swung my first leg over the fence, and then the other. All of a sudden the drop in front of me looked a lot farther than I thought it would. I was just about to swing my leg back over to think about this idea some more, when a cold little hand shoved me and I fell into the darkness, hitting the damp ground with a thump.

"Ouch! Sunny!" I shouted. "Why did you do that?"

Instead of answering me, she fell on top of me, knocking off my hanger hat. "Sunny!"

"We're really Team Smasha now," she said, giggling right into my face. "Get it, Masha?" she said. "Smash-a." The warm breath from her giggles just about smothered me. But I couldn't help myself, and I started giggling too.

I felt around for my hanger hat and stuck it back on. It was missing most of its pencils now, but I couldn't worry about that. I still had a fistful of grass, and we needed to focus on getting this knot tied and then putting this grass into the ground. I could see most of the yard around me now. Morning was on its way.

We didn't have much time left.

A Ghostly Showdown

I ran for the porch, my eyes searching for Alice and Junchao. I couldn't see them. I kept thinking, Ten more steps and they'll come into view. It was getting lighter but it was still night. They could be sitting in the moon shadow of the house.

I knew that I shouldn't have left them.

I knew that Trudy would get them if I did.

And now she had.

What had she done with them?

Maybe they were locked up in the closet? Maybe she took them to the light? How was I going to explain this to Junchao's and Alice's moms?

I swerved around the wheelbarrow and up the steps of the porch.

And there they were . . . sound asleep together like two little kittens right next to the front door—two little kittens with hangers on their heads and covered in fake jewels.

I heard Sunny's footsteps on the porch stairs behind me. I turned and gave her the "shh" sign with my finger to my lips.

We stood next to each other on the porch watching Junchao and Alice sleep.

"Are you going to wake them?" Sunny whispered.

I wanted to. I needed Alice to get me to that front hall closet. And I needed Junchao to be more afraid than I was so I could pretend I wasn't as afraid as all that.

But I knew that I couldn't.

They looked so happy asleep. There were no ghosts in their dreams. I didn't want to wake them up so that

166

they would have to join me in the place where there was a ghost. Although they did look kind of chilly.

"Come on," I said. I opened the kitchen door, and we crept inside. I went over to the big cabinet by the refrigerator. Sunny followed. I opened up the cabinet and pulled out all of my mother's tablecloths. I handed some to Sunny. She understood what I was doing.

We snuck quietly back out the door and covered Junchao and Alice with tablecloth after tablecloth until they looked like a big pile of picnics . . . warm picnics. Junchao gave a little sigh, and I saw Alice smile in her sleep. I pointed at Sunny and then myself and mouthed, "Bathroom."

The two of us tippy-toed back into the bathroom and closed the door. Then we both slumped to the floor on the pink fuzzy bathroom rug.

Sunny let out a huge yawn. I couldn't stop myself from yawning too.

"We have to finish this," I said. But all I really wanted to do was sleep, sleep, sleep.

"We have two steps left."

167

Sunny's eyes were half closed, and she peered at me through her eyelashes. "We have to go to where we think the ghost resides and tie a knot in the grass."

"The front hall closet." I sighed.

"And then we have to take the grass with the knot in it and bury it in the backyard to put the ghost back in its grave."

I closed my eyes. "But first, the front hall closet."

A bird tweeted.

I opened my eyes and stood up and looked out the bathroom window. The first red rays of the sun were poking over the horizon. It was now . . . or live with Trudy Day forever.

I turned toward the door.

"More powder?" Sunny asked.

"No," I said.

I took off my hanger hat. And then I took off all my jewelry. I placed all of it in a pile on the sink counter next to our toothbrushes.

"What are you doing?" Sunny said. "You need that stuff to stay safe."

168

"I've been scared all night long. I'm done being scared," I said.

Sunny shook her little head and then took off her hat and jewelry and put it on top of mine.

I picked the grass up off the bathroom rug and nodded at my little sister. She nodded back. We opened the bathroom door and walked out. And then we walked down the hall. And then we walked out into the living room. And then we walked past the chair. And then we walked past the piano. And then we ran back past the piano, stopping by the chair to breathe.

"I thought you weren't going to be scared?" whispered Sunny.

"I thought so too," I said. "Just give me a second."

I took in a long, slow breath, held it, and then . . .
CLOMP. CLOMP. CLOMP.

My eyes found Sunny's. "That's weird," I said. "I swear those are the same footsteps that we kept hearing all night long, and they seem to be coming from the exact same place every time."

"Well," Sunny said. "It's the same ghost."

Wooo. Wooo. Wooooo.

"And that sounds like the same howling sound. And it always seems to be coming from someplace up high at the end of the hallway."

"That's great," Sunny said. "That means the ghost is in the hall and not the closet. And we can get to the closet to tie the knot."

"Doesn't the ghost have to be in the closet for this to work?" I asked.

"No!" Sunny whispered into my face. "We just have to go to where the ghost resides and tie a knot in the grass. The ghost doesn't have to be home to do it!"

I hugged my little sister tight. I decided right then and there that I was never again going to get mad at Sunny for being smart. *Never!*

Together, we leaped from behind the chair and ran to the front hall closet. I got on my knees. "Is this close enough?"

"I think you have to be inside."

I threw my head back and gave a silent scream. And then I opened the closet door and stepped in next to my mother's rain boots and fumbled to tie the fastest knot I have ever tied in my entire life. Then I fell out of the closet on top of Sunny.

"Let's get out of here!"

We opened the front door and stumbled over each other trying to get out of the house as fast as we could. We let the storm door close on its own and ran as if the ghost were right at our heels all the way down to the mailbox.

"Where to?" I screamed into Sunny's face.

"The sandbox," Sunny shouted back.

We needed to get this knot into the earth as soon as possible.

We ran around the front of the house and through the side gate and into the backyard; the cool morning air made tears in my eyes and my hair whipped about my cheek. I didn't stop running until I hit the sandbox. Sunny was right behind me. She picked up her shovel and started digging in the dirt outside the sandbox.

"Why not in the box?"

"It said to bury it in the dirt, not in sand. Sand is mostly tiny little bits of eroded rock, while dirt is mostly organic matter. Plus, the soil around the box has a lower concentration of clay, making it less compact—"

"Just dig," I said.

She dug.

And as soon as I thought it would fit, I shoved the grass into the hole and pushed all the dirt over it. And then the two of us stood up and stomped the dirt into place. As soon as we finished, we fell over into the grass and lay panting.

We'd done it.

Sunny Sweet Is Too Scary

"Masha! Sunny! Hurry!"

I sat up, my head spinning. Where was I?

"Masha." Junchao's nose was two inches from my own. "I think a car just pulled into your driveway. We need to get Alice back inside before anyone finds out we slept outside on the back porch."

Now I knew where I was . . . in the grass by the sandbox. Sunny and I had fallen asleep.

"I'll run around the house and slow down whoever it is," said Sunny. "I'll tell them that I'm an early riser and like to be outside to watch the sun crossing the horizon, along with its accompanying atmospheric effects."

"You mean the sunrise?" asked Junchao.

"Who cares what she means, just go, Sunny!"

Junchao and I raced over to Alice on the porch. She had thrown off all the tablecloths, her eyes were wild, and her hair was sticking up all around her hanger hat. "I think my mom's here!" she cried.

"Don't worry," I told her. "Take off all your ghost protection."

Both of them ripped off their hats and jewels. Then Junchao got on one side of Alice and I got on the other and we lifted her off the porch and put her next to her crutches.

"Everything is okay. Sunny is slowing her down."

I held the kitchen door open. Alice walked to it. But before she let Junchao and me lift her up the little step and into the kitchen, she turned to me. "Trudy?"

"Gone." I smiled.

The three of us hugged. "We're so sorry we fell asleep," Alice said.

"Yes, Masha. I don't even remember doing it."

174

"No worries, guys . . . unless your mother catches us out here. And then we have lots of worries."

We hoisted Alice up the step and into the kitchen. Alice started for the living room and I ran ahead of her to lay out our sleeping bags on the living room floor. Junchao was right behind me. I got mine and Alice's out. Junchao unrolled hers.

The front door began to open. We could hear Alice's mom talking to Sunny. "That is so interesting, Sunny. So we see the sunrise before the sun actually rises."

"Yes," said Sunny. "It's called atmospheric refraction."

We threw all the pillows onto the floor just as Alice came into the living room. I hopped into my sleeping bag. Junchao plopped down into hers. And Alice was just about to when her mother walked through the door.

Alice froze.

Junchao and I blinked up from the floor.

Alice's mom smiled a huge smile. "Just getting up, lazy heads?" she said.

Sunny giggled.

Then Junchao gave her loud "HO-HO-HO."

Alice and I looked at each other and started to laugh too.

"Well, I'll help you gather your things. Your father and brother are in the car. It's going to be a beautiful day and we have a lot to do, so I hope you're not going to be too tired," she said.

Alice turned to Junchao and me so her mother couldn't see her face and frowned.

She *was* going to be too tired today.

We all were.

Ghost hunting was hard work.

Mrs. Song came into the living room, wearing her sunflower pajamas, and said hello to Alice's mother.

"Why so dirty?" Mrs. Song asked me.

I looked down. My pajamas were a mess.

"We did mud masks," Alice blurted. "See how smooth our skin is?" She blinked at her mom.

"Gorgeous," her mom said, touching Alice's cheek. "And I see you also powdered yourselves up."

"It was a beauty tip," Alice said.

"Yeah," said Junchao. "How to look stunningly pale."

"Well, it sounds like you girls had a wonderful night." Alice's mother helped me roll up sleeping bags, gather pillows, and pack clothes while Alice and Junchao headed down the hall to get dressed.

We were just about done straightening up when Junchao's mom walked in. I couldn't believe that my first sleepover was over.

Everyone headed to the front door, where Alice's wheelchair was waiting. "This was a nice success," Alice's mom said. "I don't know why I ever worried. We'll have to host the next sleepover, honey."

"REALLY?" screamed Alice, throwing her arms around her mother's waist.

"Really," repeated her mom.

"And then Junchao after that," said Junchao's mother.

The three of us smiled at one another. And then I hugged my friends good-bye.

"That was the greatest sleepover!" Alice said into my ear.

Junchao laughed. "Ho-ho-ho."

"*Xing Yun San You* forever," I said.

My friends were the best!

Mrs. Song closed the door behind everyone. "*Yóutiáo?*" she said.

"Yes! Yes! Yes!" Sunny and I screamed, jumping up and down.

Yóutiáo were these delicious donut-like sticks that Mrs. Song made every once in a while for special occasions. And Mrs. Song let Sunny and me pour sugar all over them, even though she says that they don't eat them like that in China.

My stomach growled.

"Give me twenty minutes." She laughed, and then she walked into the kitchen.

I took a huge . . . long . . . breath and fell onto the couch. Sunny crawled up next to me.

"Good work," I said.

"Good work to you too."

She leaned her head on my shoulder. I put my head back against the couch and closed my eyes.

CLOMP. CLOMP. CLOMP.

Sunny and I sat up. Then she leaped from the couch. But before she could run out of the room, there came the now way too familiar . . .

Wooo. Wooo. Woooo.

I looked at Sunny. She looked back at me. And then I knew—Sunny Sweet was the ghost all along.

"SUNNY!" I shouted, jumping off the couch . . . not even caring that my feet were right next to the place where the little men could grab me and pull me under because . . . there were no little men . . . and there was no older sister in Alice's attic that came down and played with her hair . . . and if you chewed gum at night you were just chewing gum . . . and those feet I saw in the shed under the door were most likely a bunch of rakes . . . and there was no Trudy Day in the front hall closet!

Sunny jumped behind the chair, poking her head over the top of it to watch me.

"Why did you do it this time?" I yelled. "What dumb science experiment was I a part of? Some weird sleep thing? Or a brain experiment? Or some experiment to do with seeing in the dark? What was it, Sunny? What?"

She blinked at me over the chair. "There was no experiment."

"Oh right," I said. "So you did all this for what? Just for fun?" I yelled.

Sunny stood up. She looked out the window, thinking for a minute. And then she turned to me with a look of surprise on her face. "Yes, Masha. That is why I did it. That is *exactly* why I did it."

"What?" I said.

Sunny came out from behind the chair. "I didn't know why I was doing it. The whole night I've been wondering why. At first, I just wanted you guys to be scared so you wouldn't care if I stayed up with you a little more. But then I kept doing it. And I couldn't figure out why. You already were letting me stay up. And also, I was getting pretty tired. But I kept doing it and doing it. And I kept asking myself why I was. But I didn't know. And now I know. You figured it out, Masha. I did it because it was fun. And I liked it. I liked having fun."

I sighed and fell back onto the couch.

Sunny ran to me and jumped onto my lap and hugged me tight. "Thanks, Masha. Thanks for letting me have fun with you."

How did she do it? How did she wreck my entire world and then make it completely impossible for me to kill her?

"I wish I had friends like you do," she said into my neck.

I closed my eyes and thought about Junchao and Alice. Then I kissed the top of Sunny's little head . . . I wished she did too.

"You're my friend," I whispered.

"Really," she said, yawning into my chin.

"Really," I said.

CLOMP. CLOMP. CLOMP.

I pulled the couch blanket over us and waited for the ghostly howl to come, which I now knew must be a recording and would happen in another minute or two. But I never heard it . . . because I was asleep.

Acknowledgments

As always, thank you to Kerry Sparks and Caroline Abbey for starting it all. Thank you also to Brett Wright and everyone at Bloomsbury USA Children's for taking on Sunny Sweet. And finally, thank you to my sisters for all the torture (and the love) . . . Without you, there could be no Sunny.